THE SEEDS OF HATE

by

HARRY CARMICHAEL

Published for

THE CRIME CLUB

by COLLINS 14 ST JAMES'S PLACE

LONDON

PRINTED IN GREAT BRITAIN
COLLINS CLEAR-TYPE PRESS : LONDON AND GLASGOW

To my good friends John Tasker and Harold Scott for their generous advice on insurance principles and practice without which the theme of this book could not have been conceived.

Beware the fury of a patient man

JOHN DRYDEN

CHAPTER I

ON THE NIGHT of July the ninth Betty Willcock was not thinking of murder. To her, violent death was something belonging to the Sunday papers, something that happened to people who lived in another world. They were merely names and touched-up photographs and terrible details that always seemed to her somehow to complete the pattern of an existence predestined for that kind of fate.

If Betty had been asked, that was what she would have said. But ten o'clock on a warm still night, with her world bounded by the quiet murmur of the river and the gathering dusk, was neither the time nor the place for thoughts of anything or anybody but Kenneth and herself.

. . . *When we are married. . . . I suppose it'll feel strange before I get used to people calling me Mrs. Smart. . . . Maybe we should wait until we can afford a house of our own . . . although Kenneth says the time to get married is when you're young. And after all Mother says long engagements sometimes lead to trouble . . . a girl can't be too careful. . . .*

Far-off voices threaded their way through her thoughts; from farther up the river came the distant sound of music. She snuggled closer and gave Kenneth a swift, fierce kiss that startled and almost frightened her.

He held her tightly for a moment and then let her go. In a sleepy voice, he asked, " What was that in aid of? "

" Nothing. I just love you . . . that's all."

. . . *Soon we won't need to find a sheltered place like this near the bank of the river when we want to be alone . . . soon I won't need to be embarrassed in case someone sees us lying on the grass together like this. . . . Will we still want to come here on a summer's evening, I wonder? . . .*

The dusk grew deeper. Across the river distant lights came on one by one. In the blue velvet of the sky to the east a solitary star brightened.

After the heat of a long day, the noise of a stuffy London

office, it was lovely just to lie and dream of the days that stretched ahead of them. She felt a sweet contentment. These moments were enough. Let the future take care of itself.

And so they dozed and kissed and dozed off again in each other's arms. Time drifted by like the gently flowing river.

Somewhere a clock was striking the hour when she roused to hear Kenneth saying ". . . better get a move on. It's eleven o'clock . . . I'll be late at the bakery. Got to change and make some sandwiches when I get home."

She sat up and took a comb from her handbag and began tidying her hair. It gave her something to do while she subdued the sense of disappointment she always felt when it was time for them to part. They seemed to be so much away from each other.

. . . I never thought that being in love would be like this. It's silly . . . but you're not really happy. You keep wishing that each day was to-morrow because to-morrow is one day nearer. I wonder if every girl feels like I do? . . .

Kenneth lit a cigarette and sat hugging his knees while he waited for her. When she began to rummage in her bag for a handkerchief, he said, "We'll have to hurry. I don't want the old man to think I'm taking liberties after he told me I didn't need to start work before twelve . . . and it must be well after eleven by now. Here's that fellow and his dog that we always see whenever we come here."

A man came along the footpath separating the spot where they sat from the stretch of rough grass and bushes lining the river's edge. In the near-darkness Betty recognised his build, the way he swung his stick smartly as he walked, the faint tinkle of the dog chain brushing against his leg.

He was wearing a white, open-necked shirt and the light-coloured cap he always wore. Behind him trotted the little bustling Scotch terrier that was his regular companion each time Betty had seen him taking his evening stroll along the banks of the Thames.

Man and dog went past and lost themselves in the dusk. When the sound of footsteps dwindled into the distance, Betty said, " Help me to brush the grass off my skirt. If I go home looking like this, Mother will fear the worst."

With unusual abruptness Kenneth caught hold of her and pulled her close. His kiss hurt her lips.

When she freed herself and recovered her breath, she said, " Now, what was that in aid of ? "

" Oh, I don't know. I just felt that "—he stooped to brush her skirt clumsily and then turned away so that she was unable to see his face—" we seem to spend no time at all together. The evening passes too quickly."

Betty said, " I know. I feel the same way . . . but it won't be long now, darling. We'll just have to be patient."

" I'm sick of being patient. I've got a good job and you wouldn't need to stop working until—" He broke off and put his arms round her again. " Why don't we get married right away ? "

" We can't, silly. You know perfectly well we can't."

" Why can't we ? If you loved me as you say you do you wouldn't care what anyone said."

" It isn't anything to do with what people would say. You know that."

" Then what is it ? "

She knew this mood. He wanted to be angry with someone or something, to release the feelings pent up inside him. Going on like this, seeing each other alone only once or twice a week, was not natural. It put a strain on both of them.

A character in some television play once said: *The instinct of young people in love isn't the kind of thing you can dismiss with economic arguments. Nature isn't interested in the housing situation or what people can afford. . . .*

And it was worse for a man than it was for a woman. Women had more patience. They had more self-control, too. Perhaps it was because they had so much more to lose . . . just as they had so much to give. . . .

She felt a sudden pity. With tender hands she took hold of his face and reached up to kiss him. Time no longer mattered. They loved each other: they belonged to each other. Whatever happened would be right. Whatever he wanted would be right.

With her mouth against his, she whispered, " If you want to skip work to-night, I'll stay here a little while longer with you."

His hands gripped her hard. There was hunger in the pressure of his lips, the tremble that ran through him. He was no longer the Kenneth she knew. Between them they shared a fierceness that made them strangers.

It was the furious barking of a dog that pulled them apart. Beyond the next bend in the footpath, someone cried out. There were the sounds of a struggle among the bushes.

A voice shouted, " No . . . no ! Keep away ! I'm warning you. . . ."

Kenneth said, " What the devil's going on ? Wait here, Betty. No sense in your coming, too. I'll just take a quick look in case—" Before she could stop him he had set off at a run towards the bend in the path.

In that moment while she hesitated and watched him becoming a faint running figure in the dusk the wild barking of the dog ceased abruptly. There was no further sound of a struggle, no protesting voice crying out in alarm.

For endless seconds she could hear only Kenneth's footsteps beating on the path. Then there was a distant splash as something fell heavily into the water. Farther off, a second pair of footsteps receded swiftly and were gone.

She was running after Kenneth by that time, running with the breath catching in her throat and her heart pounding hysterically. As she ran she called out, " Kenneth . . . don't go near. . . . Please, please, don't go near ! Come back . . . don't leave me. . . ."

Now she could see his vague figure not far ahead. He had stopped by the side of the path where a jumble of bushes bulked against the lesser darkness of the sky.

The other footsteps had gone. A long way off she thought she heard someone crossing the foot of Orleans Road where it flanked Marble Hill Park. She could not be sure. Her mind was filled with nothing but fear for Kenneth's safety.

By then she had almost reached the spot where he stood. As she came closer still, a thin, despairing voice began calling for help from somewhere out on the river.

Kenneth said, " I can't see a damn' thing. This is where I heard them fighting . . . somebody ran off before I could get here."

Together they pushed their way through the bushes beyond which lay a small clearing close to the water's edge. With Betty clinging to his hand he went as near as he could and stared out across the river.

The man in the water had stopped calling for help. Both of them saw him at the same moment. He was a dozen yards from the bank, only his head showing above the surface.

As they caught sight of him, he raised himself a little and cried out for the last time. Then he disappeared and the dark river rolled on with no sound except the faint chuckle of the water lapping against the bank beneath their feet.

Betty began to shiver violently. When Kenneth held her close to him, she said, " Let's get away from here . . . please . . . please . . . let's get away from here. You can't do anything. You can't—"

" I could've tried to save him," Kenneth said. " If I'd got here just a few seconds sooner. . . ."

" There wasn't anything you could do. Take me home. I'm frightened . . . the other man might come back."

" He'd be crazy if he did. We'll have to report this to the police, Betty. We can't just walk off and forget all about it."

" You can tell them whatever they want to know after you've taken me home. Please, darling. I want to get away from this place. I'll never come back here again."

Kenneth said, " O.K. O.K. I'll take you home first."

As they crossed the little clearing he was saying, ". . . I still think I might've—" then the words stuck in his throat and he halted abruptly.

In a changed voice, he said, " Stand still and don't move. I've just kicked against something and I've got to see what it is."

She hung on to him while he brought out his lighter. In its small steady flame both of them saw what it was that he had stumbled over.

Anger swept across Betty's fear. She said, " Oh, the poor thing . . . the poor little thing ! What a shame ! "

Close by their feet lay the body of the Scotch terrier, blood still oozing from a wound in its head. Caught in its grinning teeth was a torn scrap of grey cloth.

All around were the signs of a struggle. The grass had been flattened by trampling feet, a nearby bush was crushed and broken. There was blood on the grass, blood on the handle of the stout walking-stick lying not far from the body of the dog.

A renewed fit of trembling shook Betty when she caught sight of the light-coloured cap that the man had been wearing when he went past with the Scotch terrier trotting at his heels. It had all happened too suddenly for her to grasp the finality of what she had seen.

. . . *Only a few minutes ago he was alive. Now his body's floating down-river. . . . What could've made someone do a shocking thing like that ? He must be mad. . . .*

The dog chain lay on the flattened grass. Close by glinted a pair of broken spectacles. Fragments of glass winked in the light.

Kenneth said, " Whoever did this must be a maniac." The flame of his lighter went out.

Then he put his arm around her and tugged her gently away. " Come on, darling. This is no place for you."

The darkness seemed all the greater after that tiny light had gone but she thought she could still see the bloodstained cap, the walking stick with a dirty red mess on its handle, the dog grinning in death.

A surge of revulsion made her feel sick. Kenneth had blood on one of his shoes.

If she had not tempted him to make love to her again . . . if they had set off home as they had done the week before when the man with the dog had passed them on his evening walk . . . she would not have seen what happened to him.

. . . *Someone must've been lying in wait for him among*

the bushes . . . someone might've been watching Kenneth and me. It could've happened to us. If the man with the dog hadn't come along just then. . . . Maybe he was attacked by a maniac. People like that don't have any reason for what they do. How do I know he's gone ? How do I know he isn't somewhere near ? Perhaps he's hiding in those bushes over there. . . .

Panic gave a distorted meaning to every minute sound as they pushed their way through the bracken and came out on to the footpath again. She was still cold and shaken when they had left the frightening place far behind and the lights of Orleans Road were beacons of safety just ahead of them in the close, quiet darkness.

Once, she thought she heard footsteps behind them as they hurried along the street towards Richmond Road. She knew it was only imagination : she knew she was safe. Soon she would be home . . . it was not far now. In a few minutes she would be home.

But the fear remained. It was still with her when they reached the house and she had given Kenneth her key.

Then the door was open . . . and they were inside the lighted hall . . . and a familiar voice from the living-room was asking, " Is that you, Betty ? "

A flood of longing rushed over her and her legs felt suddenly very weak. As the living-room door opened, she said breathlessly, " Oh, Mum, a terrible thing has happened. . . ."

CHAPTER II

UNDER THE BRIGHT GLARE of portable floodlights, Detective-Superintendent Mullett of Scotland Yard in company with Detective-Sergeant Pugh and half a dozen constables from the local division made a painstaking search of the river bank where the affair had occurred. The spot was photographed, a sketch made showing the relative positions of the dead dog, the bloodstained walking-stick, the dog-chain half-hidden in the tall grass, the battered cap, and the broken pair of spectacles.

While a man with a sickle proceeded to cut the grass over a wide area, others examined the ground inch by inch. One result of their search was that parts of a spectacle lense were found to be missing.

The crushed frame was pieced together and the fragments of glass fitted into place. Then the ground was thoroughly scrutinised again from the bushes fringing the footpath to the edge of the river bank.

They had no more success the second time than they had had the first. The lens for the right eye was incomplete.

When a final search revealed no more pieces of glass, Sergeant Pugh said, " If I may say so, sir, it's pretty obvious what must've happened."

Superintendent Mullett straightened up from the improvised table under one of the floodlights and stretched himself. He said, " What would you say was obvious, Sergeant ? "

He was a bulky man with deep lines around the mouth and a slow voice that always seemed to convey a hint of amusement. In looks and manner he could have been a schoolmaster.

Pugh said, " The bloodstains are on the right side of the cap and it's part of the right lens that's missing. Looks as if one of the blows he was struck caught him in the right eye and drove bits of glass into his face. Judging by the amount of blood, he was hit more than once. Wouldn't you agree, sir ? "

" It would certainly account for the missing pieces of that lens. But one thing I don't understand is how he came to be battered with his own stick. According to the girl Willcock he was a well-built man who could've been expected to use the stick on someone else if he was attacked, instead of letting someone use it on him."

" Maybe it was snatched from him, sir, without warning."

" Then we'd have found his broken spectacles over there, on or beside the footpath, not here beyond the bushes. And what made him leave the path in the first place ? "

" Could've been to get hold of his dog. The poor little devil might've disturbed something—or somebody."

" Yes, that's possible. Another thought I've had "—the Superintendent looked down into the glazed eyes of the dog and then turned away—" is that the person who did this thing was known to both the man and poor Scottie there."

Sergeant Pugh thought about it solemnly before he said, " But that young fellow Smart told us the dog did a lot of barking. It wouldn't have done that if the person was somebody it knew."

" It might, Sergeant, it might. However familiar the person was, Scottie would make a fuss when his master was attacked. And before he got his head bashed in "—Mullett picked up the torn scrap of cloth and turned it over in his hands—" he managed to collect a souvenir that might make our job a lot easier."

Pugh said, " We won't get very far until we find out who his master was. Unless he went straight down and lodged on the bottom, he may be miles down river by now. The boys out there don't seem to be having much luck."

Out on the greying waters of the Thames a police launch with a searchlight mounted on its bow tacked here and there while men amidships trailed grappling lines. In a rowing boat towed by a long rope from the stern two men were similarly occupied.

Across the river a hazy dawn lightened the sky. It looked like the start of another hot day.

Superintendent Mullett stretched again. He said, " Somebody living not far from here is bound to get in touch with the police when the man of the house doesn't come back from his evening walk. Shouldn't be surprised if there's a report at the station by this time. He must have a wife or someone to get excited when they find he's been out all night."

" Even if she went to bed before he took the dog for a walk," Pugh said.

" When she wakes up she'll discover he's missing . . . what's the reason for the sudden activity over there ? "

The man with the sickle had been busily engaged chopping in the undergrowth among the bushes about twenty yards away. Now he was standing upright with something in his hand that flashed in the light of the floodlamps.

Mullett said, " Let's see what he's found. . . ."

It was a powder compact that looked more expensive than the usual run of such things. The man with the sickle said, " I came across it just this side of the bushes, sir, lying in the grass where the ground makes a kind of little bank. Caught sight of it just after I found these."

The two cigarette stubs he was holding had been only partly smoked. They were the filter tip kind. One tip was smudged with lipstick.

Superintendent Mullett said, " Thanks. Now go back and see if you can find anything else."

He squeezed one of the cigarette stubs gently between the tips of his fingers and went on almost to himself, " No telling how long they've been lying there. The dew on the grass would've kept them moist. . . . Let's have a look at that other thing."

The powder compact looked fairly new. It was ornamented in gilt and enamel and must have cost more than the average woman would have been prepared to spend. Inside the lid there was the usual mirror. The small puff looked comparatively unused and the powder container was almost full.

When he had snapped the lid shut again, Mullett turned the compact over and studied the underside with his head held back. Then he glanced up at Sergeant Pugh.

" Might've struck something here. Read the inscription engraved on it."

Pugh read aloud : " *To Cynthia on her Twenty-First Birthday. From the Office Staff of Morrison Motors.* No date, sir, but the thing looks pretty new, doesn't it ? "

" Should be interesting to hear Cynthia's explanation of how she came to lose it."

" Want me to find out something about Morrison Motors, sir ? "

" Yes, but don't show it around unless you have to. See if you can have a talk with this Cynthia and learn anything you can about the company she keeps. Meantime I'll have the lab. go to work on the walking stick and the cap and those spectacles."

The police launch abandoned its efforts after another two hours of fruitless dragging operations. By then it seemed apparent that the body of the man whom Betty Willcock and her young man had seen struggling in the water had been carried some distance down river before it lodged somewhere on the bottom. There it would remain until the gases caused by putrefaction brought it to the surface.

Superintendent Mullett told himself that the man who had taken his dog for its last walk on a pleasant summer's evening might reappear within a few days or a few weeks. It all depended on a variety of factors.

From the police point of view, identification was the more immediate problem. Someone in the neighbourhood must have known a man who had worn a light-coloured cap and who had taken a little Scotch terrier for its nightly walk. In some home not far away people must soon start worrying over what had happened to a man who should have returned before bedtime.

To tell some woman that her husband was never coming back would be the usual unpleasant task. Superintendent Mullett was not looking forward to it.

Sergeant Pugh had no difficulty tracing the firm known as Morrison Motors. It was a substantial business with several depots in the London area and a showroom in Portland Street. The head office was in Cheapside.

At nine-fifteen on the morning of July the tenth Pugh called on the office supervisor, a grey-haired woman who wore a hearing aid. She received him in a small, tidy room with glass-panelled walls on two sides and a window looking down on the sunlit thoroughfare outside.

Through the glass walls he could see three or four typists, a young woman at a telephone switchboard, and a youth operating a franking machine. A door on the other side of the general office bore a plaque with the name : *Mr. T. K. Morrison.* Painted on the frosted-glass window of an adjoining door was the word : *Cashier* and below it in smaller letters : *Mr. George Heald.*

The woman with the hearing aid said, " Would you like to take a seat ? I'm Miss Gilchrist. What is it you want to inquire about ? "

Pugh said, " We're rather anxious to get in touch with a young lady who, we believe, is employed by this company."

A slight shadow passed over Miss Gilchrist's long, pale face. She said, " No trouble—I hope ? "

" I'm only here to make inquiries about some lost property," Pugh told her.

" Oh, I see. . . . In times like these "—she folded her hands together and made a small pointed mouth—" one never knows, does one ? "

" Very true," Pugh said.

Miss Gilchrist seemed to expect him to go on. When she had waited as long as was polite, she asked, " What's the name of the young lady you'd like to speak to ? "

" We only know her Christian name. It's Cynthia."

" Indeed." Miss Gilchrist turned her head and looked out across the main office at the young woman seated at the telephone switchboard. She said, " The only Cynthia we have here is our telephonist, Miss Blake."

Pugh said, " Then she must be the one I want to see. Can you tell me how old she is ? "

" What a strange question ! Didn't you say "—Miss Gilchrist touched the collar of her high-necked blouse as though to make sure the top button had not come unfastened

—" you were making inquiries about some lost property ? "

" I did," Pugh said. In the same tone, he asked, " Do you happen to know if she recently celebrated her twenty-first birthday ? "

" Yes, about two months ago. But I'm sure I don't know how that can possibly have anything to do with lost property, Sergeant."

" You would—if I explained the circumstances. Could I speak to your Miss Blake privately for a few moments ? "

In a slightly affronted voice, Miss Gilchrist said, " Of course. . . . Would you like to use this office ? "

" Thank you very much. This will do nicely."

She stood up and fumbled with the waistband of her skirt as if her corset was biting. " Please wait here. I'll send Miss Blake in to you."

Sergeant Pugh said, " You're being very helpful. I'll do my best not to keep her too long. . . ."

Cynthia Blake was a brunette with a well-developed figure and slightly too much make-up. She said, " You wanted to see me ? " Her eyes were nervous.

Pugh said, " I'm Detective-Sergeant Pugh of Scotland Yard. I think you may be able to help me in some inquiries I'm making."

" Yes ? " Now there was a trace of fright in her eyes.

" Have you lost anything recently ? "

" I—don't think so. Why ? "

" Bccause this has come into our possession and "—he put his hand in his pocket and brought out the powder compact—" we have reason to believe it belongs to you. Would you look at it and tell me if it is your property ? "

She stared at the compact and remained silent. Her face had grown pale.

Very quietly, he prompted, " Well, Miss Blake ? "

" It—" She moistened her lips and began again. " It looks like one I used to have . . . but I don't think it's mine. As far as I know mine is at home . . ." Then her voice tailed off as he turned the compact over and showed her the underside.

He said, " It has your name engraved on it, Miss Blake. Looks as if you must be mistaken, doesn't it ? "

After she had wet her lips again, she asked, " Where did you find it ? "

" That's something I'm afraid I can't tell you just yet. What I want to know is where did you lose it ? "

She put her hands behind her back and took her eyes off the compact and looked up at him with sullen obstinacy hardening her mouth. She said, " How would I know ? I'm always losing things."

" This is quite an expensive article," Pugh said. " And it was a fairly recent gift. I'm sure you must've valued it."

" Of course I valued it. But I've lost more expensive things before now." In an aggressive tone, she added, " What's all the mystery about, anyway ? Why do the police have to question me like this because I lost my powder compact ? "

" You're the one who's making the mystery," Pugh said.

" What makes you say that ? "

" Because I think you know perfectly well where you lost it."

She pulled at her fingers and went on looking at him while she swallowed once or twice. When she had made up her mind, she said, " It isn't a crime, is it, to lose something ? "

" No."

" Supposing I do have an idea where I lost it. . . . I don't see that it's anybody else's business."

Sergeant Pugh said, " Normally, that might be so. But in this instance the circumstances of the loss are part of a police investigation. So we'd be grateful, Miss Blake, if you could see your way to co-operate with us. Beyond that I can only tell you that the matter is a very serious one."

Cynthia Blake said, " I don't know what you're talking about. I haven't done anything wrong. Just because I go and lose my compact you behave as if I'm some kind of criminal."

He returned the compact to his pocket and folded his arms. He said, " I'm sorry if I gave you that impression . . . and perhaps I'd better not keep you from your work any longer. Perhaps you need time to think it over. I'll call on you at your home outside of business hours . . . if you'll be good enough to give me your address."

In a dry voice, she said, " No . . . no, don't do that. I'd rather my family didn't get to hear. . . ." There she ran out of words.

" Get to hear what ? "

" That I went to Richmond with—someone."

" A man ? "

" Yes. My father would be furious if he knew."

" Why wouldn't he approve of your companion ? "

" You don't know what a silly question that is. Dad would have a fit if he had the slightest idea. . . ." She swallowed again.

Pugh said, " Married man ? "

With a guilty look at the people in the general office, she said, " Yes. Now you understand . . . don't you ? "

" I understand all right. What's this man's name and where can I get in touch with him ? "

" Must you ? " She seemed to be trying to pull her fingers off.

Sergeant Pugh said, " Look, Miss Blake. I've already told you this is a very serious matter. Now I must insist that you give me this man's name and address or I shall have to take steps to obtain the information by other means. Those other means will almost certainly cause you some embarrassment. If you wish to avoid that I'd advise you to tell me what I want to know. Do I make myself clear ? "

She nodded dumbly. In a small, frightened voice, she asked, " Will you have to tell—my family ? "

" Not necessarily. It all depends on what this man has to say. To start with, who is he ? "

With another glance out at the general office, she said huskily, " Mr. Heald, the cashier."

Pugh said, " I see. . . ." When a man had a teenage daughter of his own it was foolish to pass hasty judgment on someone who was little more than a schoolgirl herself. " When did you lose your powder compact ? "

" Last week-end."

" Which day ? "

" Sunday . . . Sunday evening . . . a week ago yesterday."

" Where do you believe you lost it ? "

" On the river bank at Richmond."

" Whereabouts on the river bank ? "

" Just a little way past Marble Hill Park."

" Would you know the spot again ? "

" I—I think so." A touch of colour came into her cheeks. " I didn't pay much attention at the time. We were walking and talking and we thought—we'd sit down a while."

He brought out a pocket map of the Richmond district and opened it on Miss Gilchrist's desk. He said, " Show me as near as you can the place where you sat down."

After a little hesitation, she said, " I think . . ." She nibbled at her lip and moved her forefinger here and there on the map in the area between Orleans Road and Lebanon Park. Then she said, " It was just about here." Her painted fingernail covered the spot where the body of the Scotch terrier had been found.

" Can you describe the place ? "

The colour deepened in her cheeks. " It's got some bushes that hide it from the path . . . so you can't be seen."

Once again, Sergeant Pugh said, " I see. Do you smoke, Miss Blake ? "

" Yes. Why ? "

" A couple of cigarette ends were found near your powder compact. One of them had lipstick on it that looked like the shade you use."

" Oh. . . ." She nibbled at her lip again before she asked, " What were you looking for when you found my compact ? "

" Anything we could find."

" But why ? "

" A man was drowned at that spot. We're trying to establish the circumstances of his death."

Cynthia Blake took a sudden breath. She was not quick enough to hide the fear that came into her face. Behind the fear lay some kind of realisation which interested Sergeant Pugh very much.

He waited. After a long silence, she asked, " When did it happen ? "

" Last night. Would you mind telling me where you were about eleven o'clock ? "

" At home. I didn't go out at all last night." She was more startled than frightened by the question.

" When was the last time you went out with Mr. Heald ? "

" On that Sunday evening—a week ago."

" You haven't been with him since then ? "

" No." With a fresh hint of stubbornness tightening her mouth, she added, " I don't intend to see him again, either. I told him so that Sunday." The recollection of something disturbing showed momentarily in her eyes.

Pugh said, " What made you decide not to see him again ? "

" Something happened that night that—upset me. I suddenly realised how easy it would be for people to find out I was going around with a married man."

" What caused you to be upset ? "

" We discovered a man spying on us. George—Mr. Heald, I mean—says he was one of those Peeping Toms. I got frightened in case Mr. Heald caught him and there'd be a fight. That was when "—she moved restlessly—" I made up my mind I wasn't going out with him any more."

" Did Mr. Heald chase this man ? "

" Yes, but he got away."

" Was Mr. Heald very angry ? "

" He got pretty wild about it. I was afraid—" She stopped short and looked down at her hands. With obviously assumed indifference, she went on, " Anyway, he didn't catch him . . . so it doesn't matter."

Sergeant Pugh said, " Do you happen to know if you're the only girl Mr. Heald's been taking out ? "

Cynthia Blake was neither surprised nor annoyed by the question. With a shrug, she said, " I don't suppose I am . . . and I don't care either way. George is popular with the girls. He's not mean and he gives you a good time."

Pugh remembered his own daughter and a slow anger

stirred among his thoughts. He said, " Now you've decided that all good times come to an end. Any idea how Mr. Heald spent last night ? "

She shrugged again. " Outside the office I haven't spoken to him since that Sunday. I've already told you that . . . more or less."

" So you have. By the way, why didn't you go back to look for your compact if you knew where you'd lost it ? "

" I haven't had the opportunity . . . and I didn't fancy wandering about there alone after what had happened, in any case."

" Very wise, Miss Blake." Pugh folded the map and put it in his pocket and gave her a long, straight look. " I hope you'll be equally wise when it comes to talking to Mr. Heald after I leave here. I shall be questioning him shortly and I don't want him to know in advance what my questions are going to be. You understand what I mean, don't you ? "

" Yes. Yes, I understand. Can I go now ? "

" When you've told me one thing more. Would anyone in the office become curious if the cashier went out for a little while ? "

" I don't think so. Sometimes he has to go to the showroom . . . or one of the depots. Why d'you ask ? "

Sergeant Pugh said, " Because I'm hoping you've learned your lesson, young woman. I don't want to create any talk either here or at your home. Now, I suggest you get back to your work."

She nodded and went to the door. There she turned and asked, " What do I say if any of the girls start asking questions ? "

" You should've thought of that before, shouldn't you ? "

" Can I tell them I left my compact in a ladies' room somewhere . . . and that's why you've been talking to me ? "

" Since you certainly won't tell them the truth," Pugh said, " one lie won't do any more harm than another. . . ."

When she had returned to the switchboard, he went out

without seeing Miss Gilchrist again. As the lift carried him down to the ground floor he was once more thinking of his own daughter.

From a telephone kiosk at the corner of Moorgate he phoned Morrison Motors and asked to speak to Mr. George Heald. While he waited he told himself he should have questioned Heald before he left the premises.

There was no guarantee that Cynthia Blake would not blab the whole story to Heald as soon as she thought it was safe. Sentiment was a luxury that no copper could afford.

. . . Still . . . maybe she was telling the truth. And maybe she comes from a decent family. Pity if a silly girl were to get nice people mixed up in a nasty business. . . .

Then a man's voice said, "Yes ? This is George Heald."

Pugh said, "I'm speaking for Detective-Superintendent Mullett of Scotland Yard. My name is Pugh, Sergeant Pugh. The Superintendent would like you to call at his office as soon as possible, Mr. Heald, preferably right away."

Heald said, "I don't understand. Why should anyone at Scotland Yard want to see me ? "

"We are investigating the death of a man who was drowned in the Thames at Richmond and we have reason to believe you may have some information that will help us in our inquiries."

In a pained voice that was a little too loud, Heald said, "But I don't know anything about a man who was drowned at Richmond."

"Perhaps not, sir. Nevertheless, we know you were in that neighbourhood recently. The Superintendent would be obliged if you would call on him so that he may ask you a few questions."

After a brief pause, Heald asked, "How do you know where I was recently ? "

"A young lady told us, a young lady called Cynthia Blake. I understand you are acquainted with her ? "

"Any reason why I shouldn't be ? She's a member of our office staff."

"Quite so, sir. But this has nothing to do with the

office. She has informed me that she was in your company on the river bank at Richmond last Sunday evening. That is, a week ago last night."

"You make it sound like a crime, Sergeant, for a man to take a girl for a walk."

"I'm sorry about that, sir. It's not my place to pass any opinion on the company either you or Miss Blake keeps. It's the fact that you were recently in the vicinity of Marble Hill Park that may be important."

After another short silence, Heald said, "Why didn't you visit me here at the office instead of phoning me like this?"

"Interviewing you after I'd just spoken to Miss Blake might've encouraged a certain amount of gossip," Pugh said. "I had no wish to create a scandal."

"Very nice of you, Sergeant, I'm sure. You seem a decent sort of bloke. What is all this about, anyway?"

"Superintendent Mullett is the man to tell you that, sir. Can I tell him you'll be calling on him soon?"

Heald took a few seconds to make up his mind. Then he said, "You can tell your Superintendent that I'll be on my way to see him inside the next ten minutes."

CHAPTER III

BEFORE TEN A.M. two people resident in the neighbourhood lying between Orleans Road and Lebanon Park, Richmond, had already come forward with information concerning the man in the light-coloured cap. His identity was still unknown, but it was now apparent that his home had been either in or near Sion Road.

A woman who lived not far from the corner of Sion Road and Riverside informed the local police that the man with the little Scotch terrier had passed her on several occasions, always at the same time each night. A girl in domestic service reported that she had seen a man of his description when she was returning home one night during the previous week after her evening off.

What puzzled Superintendent Mullett was that no one had so far notified the police about a man missing from home. He was still worrying about it when George Heald was shown into his office.

Heald was a good-looking man in his middle thirties with an Air Force tie and an over-confident manner. He accepted the Superintendent's invitation to take a seat, crossed his legs carefully so as not to spoil the crease in his well-pressed trousers, and then asked if it was all right if he smoked.

When he had lit a cigarette, he said, " On my way over here I was thinking about what your Sergeant told me on the phone. I hope there isn't going to be any unpleasantness ? "

Mullett said, " What kind of unpleasantness, Mr. Heald ? " He had no liking for the man. Heald was a type that was all too common.

Fortunately or unfortunately, there was no law against the kind of life he chose to live . . . unless his wife brought divorce proceedings. That was not always very easy.

. . . *Many a woman tolerates almost endless humiliation for the sake of her children . . . or because she's got religious objections to divorce. Some women believe that any kind of marriage is better than no marriage at all.* . . .

George Heald was saying ". . . know how people are inclined to talk, Superintendent. You only need to go for a walk with a nice-looking girl and they're ready to jump to conclusions."

Superintendent Mullett told himself they were all the same. He said, " If I may quote Shakespeare, Mr. Heald, perhaps some lines from Richard III would apply equally as well to your case as to so many others I've come across : *My conscience hath a thousand several tongues, And every tongue brings in a several tale, And every tale condemns me for a villain.* . . . In case you're interested, the quotation is from Act 5."

In a voice of controlled anger, Heald said, " Conscience has nothing to do with it, but I can't stop you thinking what you please. Apart from anything else, my friendship with Miss Blake is no concern of the police."

" None whatsoever," Mullett said. " I'm only concerned with what happened last Sunday evening a week ago when you chased a man you thought was a Peeping Tom. What did he look like ? "

" Just a man. I only caught a glimpse of him. He was off like a rabbit soon's he saw me coming towards him . . . and it was nearly dark at the time, too."

" Could you see if he was wearing a hat or a cap ? "

" No, I don't remember. I've a feeling he was bare-headed but I couldn't be sure."

" How tall would you say he was ? "

" Average height. What's he done to make you so interested in his description ? "

" That's what I'm trying to find out, Mr. Heald. I'm hoping you may be able to help me. Did you see or hear anything of a dog, a small Scotch terrier, when you chased this man from the place where you and Miss Blake were " —the Superintendent's hesitation was very slight—" resting on the grass ? "

If Heald resented the implication he showed no sign of it. With a set face, he said, " No, I didn't see any dog."

" What time did this affair take place ? "

" Must've been about eleven o'clock, I'd say. We were about to leave."

" Had anything like that ever occurred previously ? "

" You mean—at that same spot ? "

" That is precisely what I mean."

Heald moved his shoulders uncomfortably. He said, " As far as I remember that kind of thing has never happened to me before, either there or anywhere else."

Superintendent Mullett stroked his chin and looked at him steadily. Then he asked, " Has it happened to you since, Mr. Heald ? "

A new awareness came into Heald's face. He said, " I don't know what you're driving at."

" Don't worry about my thought processes : try answering my question instead."

" I don't understand your question so I can't answer it."

" Then I'll phrase it more simply. Have you been troubled by the activities of a Peeping Tom on your visits to that spot since the Sunday night we're talking about ? "

" I haven't been there since that Sunday night. Miss Blake will confirm that if you don't believe me."

" Whether I believe you or not is quite immaterial—for the moment. According to a statement made by Miss Blake when questioned by Sergeant Pugh less than an hour ago, she hasn't been in your company since a week ago last night—socially, that is. Was she telling the truth ? "

Heald shifted uncomfortably again. He said, " Yes, it's true."

" Then for all she knows, you could've taken a walk along the river bank at that spot with another young woman . . . couldn't you ? "

" Perhaps I could," Heald said roughly. " But I didn't. Sunday was the last time I was anywhere near there."

" Where do you live, Mr. Heald ? "

" Putney. Number 14a Woodberry Avenue, Putney, S.W.15."

" Thank you, Mr. Heald. I'll make a note of that."

Superintendent Mullett did so, writing in a leisurely hand in a notebook that he took from a drawer in his desk. When he had finished he laid notebook and pen on his clean, unused blotting pad and asked, " Were you at home all yesterday evening ? "

Indecision showed in Heald's eyes. He said, " If I tell you the truth, you won't go talking to my wife, will you ? "

" Not if it is the truth. Your extra-marital relationships are no concern of the police."

" Well, when I got home last night "—behind Heald's resentment there was an air of discomfort that he was unable to conceal—" I did a bit of gardening and played with the kids until it was their bedtime. After supper, the next-door neighbour came in to ask my wife about some knitting pattern . . . and they got talking." With a weak attempt at a smile, he added, " You know what women are."

" Go on," Mullett said. His inner thought was that he would rather have an honest-to-God crook any time than a man like George Heald.

" That must've been about half past eight. When I saw they were settling down for a good old chinwag I decided they could do without me . . . so I went out for a drink."

" Where did you go ? "

" The Westlea Arms. It's a pub near where I live."

" Did you stay there for the rest of the evening ? "

" No. The beer seemed to be a bit off so I thought I'd try somewhere else for a change. It was a nice night and " —he tried another smile without any more success—" I had nothing better to do."

" What time did you leave the Westlea Arms ? "

" About nine o'clock . . . I think." Quite suddenly Heald's restraint broke. He said angrily, " Look here, Superintendent. All I know so far is that some bloke was drowned last night near the place where I sat for a few minutes with Cynthia Blake last Sunday. What one thing has to do with another beats me. Don't you think I'm entitled to know why I'm being asked to account for every minute of my time ? "

Very mildly, the Superintendent said, " There's no real reason why you shouldn't know. It'll be in the newspapers sooner or later, anyway. Murder always invites a certain amount of morbid publicity."

A shocked look came into Heald's good-looking face. He said, " Murder ? D'you mean the man wasn't drowned?"

" Oh, it's pretty obvious he was drowned all right. But, before he entered the water, he received at least one blow on the head from a heavy stick and was probably only semi-conscious."

" Good God . . . surely you don't think that "—Heald ran a hand through his hair and stared at Mullett blankly —" I had anything to do with it ? Why on earth should I want to kill someone I didn't even know ? "

" He might've been playing Peeping Tom again," Mullett said. " And this time you managed to catch him."

George Heald sat opening and shutting his mouth while he thought of something to say. He looked deflated and shaken.

At last, he said, " You've got it all wrong, Superintendent.

I haven't been anywhere near that spot since that Sunday evening. I'm willing to swear to it. You've got to believe me."

"Had you ever been there before last Sunday ?"

"Yes . . . once or twice. But not since then. I didn't fancy the idea that there might be a snooper in the neighbourhood."

"And you didn't go out to Richmond last night ?"

"I keep telling you I haven't been there since a week last Sunday. I went across to Fulham after I left the Westlea Arms."

"Where did you go in Fulham ?"

"The Green Bottle in Hurlingham Road. I pop in there now and again . . . but not very often. Last night was the first time in quite a few weeks."

"Did you see anyone you knew ?"

"No. It seemed to be a quiet night there."

"Does the landlord know you ?"

"Only as an occasional customer. I didn't see him, anyway. It may have been his night off."

"How long did you stay in the Green Bottle ?"

"Until about—a quarter past ten . . . at a rough guess."

"Did you speak to anyone at all ?"

"Yes, I got into conversation with a girl. We had a couple of drinks together."

"Do you know her name ?"

"No. Never saw her before. She was alone and so was I . . . you know how it is in a pub."

"Think she'd remember you as the man she had a drink with—if ever it should be necessary for us to trace her ?"

In a tone of weak exasperation, Heald said, "It won't be necessary—take it from me. How would I know if she'd remember a man she had a drink with ?"

"Depends what you talked about," Mullett said. "Was she still in the Green Bottle when you left ?"

Heald squeezed one hand in the other and wriggled again. When his eyes at last met the Superintendent's, he said, "No . . . I took her home."

With no change of tone, Mullett said, "Let's not beat about the bush, Mr. Heald. Was she a prostitute ?"

As if he had been prodded with something sharp, Heald sat up straight and said, " Not on your life ! I don't go with women of that kind."

Superintendent Mullett sighed. " Why do men like you think they lose caste if they pay for their questionable pleasures ? . . . Dear, dear. . . . However, where did this woman live ? "

" Somewhere off Varna Road . . . up near the top end."

" Can't you be a little more specific than that ? "

" No, I wasn't paying much attention. And it was dark by the time we got there."

" Surely not, Mr. Heald, if you left the Green Bottle at ten-fifteen ? "

After some hesitation, Heald said, " We didn't go straight to her house. We called at another pub on the way." Now his hands were shaking slightly.

" What was the name of this other pub ? "

" I don't know. I've never been there before."

" Pity. . . . What time did you reach the house where this woman lived ? "

" Must've been about eleven o'clock . . . or a little later."

In a changed voice, Mullett said, " There seem to be a lot of things that you either don't know or about which you are not sure, Mr. Heald. You can't tell me this woman's name or address ; you can't tell me the name of the public house you visited after you left the Green Bottle ; now you aren't sure what time it was when you reached the woman's home. Not at all satisfactory, is it ? "

" But it's the truth nevertheless," Heald said. He was beginning to sweat. " Would it do me any good to tell lies in view of what's happened ? "

" No good at all. I'm glad you appreciate that. . . . Did you go into the house ? "

" Yes. She invited me in for a cup of coffee."

" Was anyone else there ? . . . or were you alone together ? "

" We were alone. She told me she was separated from her husband."

" Another member of the great legion of lonely women,"

Mullett said. " How much time did you spend in the house ? "

" Half an hour or so. And you're wrong in what you're thinking. It wasn't like that at all. We sat and chatted and had a cup of coffee and . . ." Heald waved one hand aimlessly. " That was all."

Superintendent Mullett said, " If my thoughts showed in my face, I'm sorry. In my job a man tends to expect the worst, human nature being what it is. However. . . . What time did you get home to Putney ? "

" About twenty past twelve or thereabouts."

" Wife waiting up for you ? "

" No, she was asleep."

" So she doesn't know when you got in . . . m-m-m ? "

With another momentary spasm of anger, Heald said, " I've told you when I got in. Everything I've told you is the truth. That's where I went and that's how I spent the evening. I don't know a damn' thing about the man who was drowned last night and "—he swallowed and took a deep breath—" if it wasn't that I don't want my wife to be upset I wouldn't have answered half your questions. I wasn't obliged to do so."

Mullett said, " For a man who has such consideration for his wife, Mr. Heald, you keep very peculiar company. Now, I think that is all for the present. I'll let you know if and when I have any further questions to ask."

" And maybe I'll let you know whether or not I'm prepared to answer them," Heald said. " There comes a limit, you know." He was white round the mouth with anger.

" Let's worry about that when we reach it," Superintendent Mullett told him. " Thank you for calling on me so promptly . . . and good day to you. . . ."

CHAPTER IV

Laboratory tests revealed the presence of both human and animal blood on the handle of the walking-stick. Hairs from the Scotch terrier were found adhering to the wood. There were also a few human hairs classified as belonging to a man of fair complexion, probably in his early forties, and greying slightly. Samples taken from the walking-stick, the broken spectacle lens and the battered cap belonged to the same blood group.

Inquiries in the neighbourhood of Marble Hill Park continued. Reports of all missing persons in the London area were carefully checked and a number of leads investigated, in every case without success.

No one came forward with information to establish the identity of the man who had called for help before he disappeared in the Thames. Neither he nor his little dog seemed to have been missed by family or friends.

During the course of that first day Detective-Superintendent Mullett received a textile report on the scrap of cloth that had been found in the Scotch terrier's jaws. It was a light-weight grey flannel of cheap quality and had apparently been torn from a trouser leg, judging by indications of a crease.

The battered and bloodstained cap the man had worn was one of many thousands made in a London factory and sold in hundreds of shops throughout the south of England. It bore no distinguishing marks to help identify its owner.

Superintendent Mullett's inquiries went on. If he had been asked he would have said that this was one of those jobs where results could not be expected overnight—if at all.

Three days went by. Then a woman phoned the local police station in Crown Road, Richmond, and reported that she had just returned home and discovered that her husband was missing.

Her name was Alice Mitchell and she lived at Number 9 Douglas Crescent, off Sion Road. For the past few days she had been visiting friends in Catford. She had expected her husband to be at home when she returned, as it was half-day closing in his business and he should have been awaiting her. From the look of the house it had been empty for some time.

. . . Yes, they kept a dog—a Scotch terrier. . . . She was sure something must have happened to her husband . . . otherwise he would have left a note to tell her where he had gone. . . .

The local inspector called on Mrs. Mitchell at Number 9 Douglas Crescent and asked a few questions. Then he got in touch with Superintendent Mullett.

Mrs. Alice Mitchell was a quiet colourless woman whose face reminded Mullett of the Victorian miniature his grandmother had worn pinned to the bodice of her stiff black dress—an emotionless woman who could have been any age between forty and fifty.

It was curiosity more than distress that showed in her remote and tranquil eyes when the Superintendent described what they had found on the river bank, and then gave her a shortened account of what he had been told by the young couple who had seen the man in the water.

While he was speaking, she sat with her gloved hands folded placidly on her lap, her eyes drifting occasionally from his face to the window looking out on Crown Road and then concentrating on his mouth as though she understood better by watching his lip movements. She never moved once all the time he was talking to her.

When he came to the end, she said, " Frank always wears a light fawn cap . . . and he carries a stick when he takes Alexander for a walk." Her voice was not that of a woman who had just learned that her husband had been brutally murdered.

With a strange thought stirring in his mind, Superintendent Mullett asked, " What is your husband's full name and age, Mrs. Mitchell ? "

" Frank Albert. He's forty-three—nearly forty-four."

" And his description ? "

" Oh, he's a fair height . . . got a good appearance. Gone a bit grey recently or he wouldn't look anything like his age. It's his good colour that's kept him looking so young."

" Does he wear glasses ? "

" Yes. Mostly for reading, though."

" Clean shaven ? "

" Yes . . . he hasn't got a moustache or anything like that." As if anxious to be helpful, she added, " In the past few months I've thought his hair's been receding a little bit at the temples, but he says it's my imagination. . . ." Her calm voice hushed as though there was something still left unsaid but she was afraid of talking too much.

" What does he do for a living ? "

With what could have been a touch of middle-class pride, she said, " He's in business for himself. We've got a tobacco and fancy goods shop in Talbot Street." Her hands moved and went still again. " I knew something was wrong when I was told it'd been shut for several days."

Mullett's sense of unreality deepened. Either this woman had no feelings or she had not yet grasped the full implications of what had happened. There was another possibility, of course, but that had no justification—yet.

He said, " Have you any family, Mrs. Mitchell ? "

She unfolded her hands and laid them side by side on her lap and glanced down at them for a moment. Then she looked at the window before she said, " No . . . we have never had any children."

" How long have you lived at Number 9 Douglas Crescent ? "

" Only a few months. We used to live over the shop but I wanted to keep a dog and there was no proper accommodation. Besides, we both thought that a house near the river would be nice . . . and we'd have a garden, too. . . ."

Once more she left the sentence incomplete. Once more she seemed to want the Superintendent to form his own impression.

Mullett said, " You don't appear to be very well known

in the district where you now live, Mrs. Mitchell. Of course, you haven't had much time to become acquainted with the neighbours, have you ? "

" No." She turned her hands over, palms down, and studied the backs of her gloves. Then she looked up and her eyes met his. In the same unchanging voice, she said, " My husband and I like to keep ourselves to ourselves. We haven't got many friends."

" Among the people you do know, Mrs. Mitchell, is your husband well liked ? "

" Yes, I think so. He's not the sociable sort. Doesn't go out much. Fond of his garden . . . and makes things at home when the weather's not fit to work out of doors."

She linked her fingers and gave the Superintendent a small, sad smile. " Frank's never been a very robust man. Nothing particularly wrong with him but just. . . ." Her smile lingered on without any meaning.

Superintendent Mullett said, " Now, there's one question, Mrs. Mitchell, that I have to ask. Have you any reason to believe that he might've made some enemy ? "

" No, he isn't the kind of man to make enemies. We've been married nearly fifteen years and I've seldom known him to have words with anyone."

" When was the last occasion ? "

" Funny you should ask that." Her eyes travelled to the window and came slowly back to Mullett's face. " He had a bit of a row with our next-door neighbour not long ago. Some people don't like dogs, you know."

" Was the trouble over your Scotch terrier ? "

" Yes. He can be very naughty "—she caught her breath and her eyes told Mullett that she was thinking of the dog with its skull crushed in—" whenever he's left alone in the house. Barks and whines each time he hears anyone passing the gate. Mr. Ogden—the man next door—complained about it once or twice not long after we went to live there. My husband said he was making a fuss about nothing . . . but we promised we wouldn't leave Alexander alone any more than we could help."

" Did this man Ogden have reason to complain again ? "

" Well . . ." She hunched her shoulders. " We have

to go out some time . . . and what happened wouldn't have been so serious if it wasn't that he just doesn't like dogs."

"Same trouble again?"

"No, this time he said Alexander had ruined his dahlias. Seems that somebody's dog had been scratching among them and dug up half his best plants. He was very angry and threatened to do all sorts of things."

Mullett said, "I see . . . Were these threats directed against your husband or the dog—or both?"

Mrs. Mitchell drew a long slow breath. For the first time since the start of the interview something close to concern showed in her eyes. She said, "I don't think the thing's worth taking too seriously. I haven't anything against Mr. Ogden apart from the fact that he made himself unpleasant over Alexander. The things he said were what you would expect a man to say when he loses his temper. Besides"—she took another deep breath and seemed to brace herself—"the man who was attacked on the river bank the other night might not have been my husband."

"I'm afraid you have to face the situation that it was your husband," Mullett said. "There isn't much doubt he was attacked by someone, struck on the head with his own stick, and then either fell or was pushed into the river. The young couple who ran to the spot just too late, saw him drown. I'm sorry."

She nodded once or twice, her face set. Nothing of what was going on in her mind revealed itself. Mullett would have sworn that her chief feeling was one of relief now that they had passed the point where she could have been expected to show some measure of shock.

At last, she said, "I just can't believe it. Poor Frank. . . . It's not right, it's not right at all. He never did anyone a bad turn in his life. . . ."

There were no tears in her eyes, no emotion in her voice. Mullett asked himself how any woman could live for fifteen years with a man and be so completely unmoved by his death.

He had known of many marriages that had bred hate

instead of love: the divorce courts were full of them day after day. But Mrs. Mitchell betrayed neither love nor hate. She had just no feeling at all. . . .

It was then that he recognised her for what she was—a stupid woman. He reminded himself that cunning and stupidity often go hand in hand. Cruelty was sometimes born in such conditions, too.

He said, "You have my sympathy, Mrs. Mitchell. This is a very bad business indeed. Where will you be if I want to get in touch with you again? I don't suppose you'll want to live in that house of yours alone just yet awhile."

"No . . . no, I wouldn't want to do that."

"Perhaps you'll go back and stay with the friends you visited in Catford?"

"That would hardly be fair to them. I'd feel I was imposing."

"Have you no family, no relatives at all, someone who could keep you company until you got settled down and had time to decide what to do?"

"Only a brother. He lives in rooms somewhere near King's Cross. Never got married . . ." She seemed almost inclined to pursue the topic of her brother's bachelor existence but the effort was too much.

Superintendent Mullett said, "Why not get him to come and live with you for the time being?"

"I can't." Her eyes crept to the window and then lost themselves somewhere on the way back. "He's a restaurant car attendant on the railway . . . so he's away from home a lot." With another little nod, she added, "I think I'd better go home until I've made up my mind. I'll have to get used to living alone, anyway." She sounded brighter at the prospect.

"So long as I know where you are," Mullett said.

"Yes. If you want me, Superintendent, that's where I'll be."

"I hope I won't need to trouble you." He wondered whether she would have maintained her composure if she could have read his thoughts.

She stood up and went to the door and then paused as though thinking. Without looking up, she said, "I don't suppose it would've made any difference if I hadn't been away from home the night—it happened."

Mullett said, " No difference at all." With no change of tone, he went on, " That reminds me. To complete my notes I'd better have the name and address of your friends in Catford . . . if you don't mind."

" Their name is Ward. They're sisters and they live at 6 Rundlesdown Avenue." As if she wanted to complete some thought before it was lost, she went on, " I went to school with the older one, Margaret. They never got married . . . but it didn't make any difference when I did. We've always remained friends."

The Superintendent said, " Thank you, Mrs. Mitchell. Just one thing more before you go. . . ."

" Yes ? "

" You told me your next-door neighbour—this man Ogden—uttered some threats when his dahlias were spoiled, but you didn't say what he threatened to do. Were these threats directed against your husband ? "

" Not from what I heard."

" What did you hear ? "

" After he'd argued with Frank for a while and both of them were beginning to lose their tempers, Mr. Ogden said if it happened again we'd know what to expect."

" By that, what did you think he meant ? "

Mrs. Mitchell opened the door and turned to look back. Her round sedate face was vaguely troubled. She said, " It was the kind of thing no one should say whether he likes dogs or not. I'm sure he couldn't have meant it."

" Couldn't have meant what ? "

" He threatened that, if it happened again "—her hand felt for the edge of the door and she seemed impatient to leave—" he would see it was the last time it did happen."

" How would he see to that ? "

" If he caught our dog in his garden again he'd beat its head in," Mrs. Mitchell said.

CHAPTER V

SERGEANT PUGH agreed it could do no harm and they might as well call now while they were in the district. Then he added, " He'd have to be mad, of course, but there's no knowing what a man will do when he gets a bee in his bonnet."

" Or a dog in his dahlias," Mullett said.

" There was obviously no love lost between the Scotch terrier and this fellow Ogden. Suppose Ogden was enjoying a stroll that same evening and he bumped into Mitchell taking Alexander for a walk . . . ? "

" If that is so, the rest isn't difficult to imagine . . . so long as we don't let our imagination run away with us."

" Alexander bites a piece out of Ogden's trouser leg," Pugh said. " Ogden grabs Mitchell's stick, either to defend himself or to get some of his own back. . . . You remember, sir, what that young couple heard Mitchell shout ? "

" Yes, I remember. The words he used were : ' No . . . no ! Keep away ! I'm warning you. . . .' They fit your supposition, Sergeant, in the circumstances. However, we'll see what Mr. Ogden has to say for himself. . . ."

Numbers 9 and 11 Douglas Crescent were adjoining semi-detached houses, one painted green-and-cream, the other in pale blue-and-white. Both had small front lawns, wooden gates and neatly trimmed privet hedges shielding the downstairs windows from the view of passersby. Both had well-tended flower beds making a colourful display.

In the case of Number 11 someone had recently been using a watering can. The soil in the garden of Number 9 looked parched after a week's hot dry weather.

Superintendent Mullett wondered if Mrs. Mitchell had returned home following her interview with him. There was no sign of life behind the curtains of either the downstairs or upstairs windows.

. . . *Of course, she may have gone shopping first* . . . *or called in on a friend. But she's scarcely the type of woman to pay an unexpected visit. Judging from what she said her only friends are the two sisters who live in Catford.*

What does a woman in her situation do with herself ? Until we recover her husband's body she can't even hold the funeral. . . . Wonder why they ever married each other ? If she isn't downright glad that he's dead she's certainly not breaking her heart. That much stands out a mile. . . .

With Sergeant Pugh close behind him he opened the gate of Number 11 and walked up the short tarmac path. Inside the porch, he said, " Looks like there's nobody at home here, either."

There was a bellpush but the spring had gone and the button was stuck fast. Mullett knocked on the leaded-glass panel of the door, waited a few seconds and knocked again.

Pugh said, " Wrong time of the day to catch a man at home, I suppose, sir. His wife should be able to tell us—"

The sound of footsteps not far off stopped him. Someone coughed as the steps drew near. Then the door opened.

Superintendent Mullett said, " Mr. Ogden ? "

" Yes." He was a small sharp-looking man with aggressive blue eyes and a hard mouth. There was nothing more than ordinary curiosity in his face as he stood looking up at them.

" My colleague and I are policemen," Mullett told him. " We are investigating the death of your next-door neighbour at Number 9. You've heard what's happened to him, I expect ? "

" Yes, I've heard. Very unpleasant affair." He glanced at Pugh, put his hands in his trouser pockets, and repeated, " Very unpleasant."

Mullett asked, " Could we, perhaps, come in for a few minutes and get you to tell us a little about him ? "

Ogden said, " I don't know anything at all about him . . . but you can come in if you wish. . . ."

With his hands still in his pockets he ushered them into a room that looked out on to the front garden—a room that was barely large enough for its pretentious furniture. The only clear space was in front of the fireplace—four or five square yards between the hearth and a table with massive ball legs.

When they had found positions for themselves, Ogden said, " Well, what was it you wanted to know ? "

" Did you see Mr. Mitchell at all that night ? "

" No, I haven't seen anything of him for the past couple of weeks."

" According to Mrs. Mitchell, she and her husband came to live here only a few months ago. They seem to have been retiring sort of people, so you wouldn't have much chance to get really acquainted."

Very coldly, Ogden said, " Whether I had the chance or not is immaterial. I certainly didn't have the inclination." He took one hand from his pocket, pulled at his ear, and gave Mullett a lopsided smile. " If you've already spoken to Mrs. Mitchell she'll have told you how I feel about people who put dogs and cats before human beings."

" She did say something about a row you'd had with her husband . . . and that's why we're here. What kind of man would you say he was—apart from this question of the trouble over his dog ? "

" Since he came to live next door "—Ogden's sharp blue eyes glanced at Pugh inquiringly—" I've only spoken to the man twice, both times on the subject of his dog. He thought more of that animal than he did of his wife."

" Are you saying that merely as a figure of speech ? "

Ogden concentrated on the Superintendent and looked mildly puzzled. " Why ? It's not such an extravagant thing to say, is it ? You know what dog-lovers are as well as I do."

" Did he have trouble with any of his other neighbours ? "

" I wouldn't be surprised. That dog of his must've wakened quite a few people around here before it was time for them to get up in the morning."

" But that's only an assumption on your part, of course."

" They didn't come and tell me they'd complained, if that's what you mean. And I don't see how all this has anything to do with what happened the other night."

" It may well have some bearing," Mullett said. " We're of the opinion that he was killed by someone who was personally known to him . . . or who at least was aware of his habits."

A look of alertness came into Ogden's eyes. He said, " You mean—someone around here ? "

" Possibly. When did you know that the man who'd been attacked on the river bank was Mr. Mitchell ? "

" Not until this morning."

" How did you get to know then ? "

" Mrs. Mitchell saw me in the garden and asked me if I'd seen anything of her husband during the past day or so. That was when I added up what I'd read in the papers and realised that the man who was drowned must've been Mitchell."

" Hadn't it struck you before ? Your next-door neighbour is missing, the dog hasn't done any barking for several days, and you read in the papers about a man and a Scotch terrier being killed not far from here while taking their evening walk. Wasn't the connection pretty obvious ? "

Ogden stopped pulling at his ear and put his hand in his pocket again. With a slight narrowing of his eyes, he said, " I don't know what you're trying to get me to say. Do you think someone killed Mitchell because he allowed his dog to become a damn' nuisance . . . me, for instance ? "

Superintendent Mullett said, " I wouldn't go as far as to say that. These are just exploratory questions. However, it is possible that Mitchell met someone he knew that night and the dog might've attacked this person who, perhaps, picked up a stone to defend himself. Mitchell tried to use his stick to protect his dog, there was a struggle during which the stick was wrenched from him and used on both him and his dog . . . with most tragic results."

" Very interesting," Ogden said. " Very interesting." This time his crooked smile was shared between the Superintendent and Sergeant Pugh. " Either of you gentlemen mind if I make a suggestion ? "

" Not at all," Mullett said.

" Well, in view of what you say, Mister. . . . I don't think you told me your name."

" I'm Detective-Superintendent Mullett. This is Sergeant Pugh."

" All right, Superintendent, here's a thought for you.

Stop worrying about the dog and concentrate instead on somebody who had a real reason for quarrelling with Mitchell. Because his dog was killed doesn't prove that it provided a motive for his death. It just happened to be there at the time, that's all."

" Do you know of anyone with whom he quarrelled recently ? "

" Yes, in a way, I do. But "—his smile vanished and he shook his head—" I'm not going to start making allegations that either of them murdered him."

" I'm not asking you to make allegations, Mr. Ogden. All I'd like you to give me is whatever information you have about any quarrels he had recently. I can promise you I won't disclose the source of the information."

Ogden said, " Whether you do or not doesn't worry me in the slightest degree. So long as I tell the truth I'm never afraid of the consequences. My wife says I believe in nothing but black or white and no half-way grey in between. Maybe she's right. I haven't much time for people who sit astride the fence."

Mullett said, " Perhaps the world would be a less complicated place if we had a few diplomats who practised your philosophy. Now. . . . What is the story about the people you say quarrelled with Mr. Mitchell ? "

When he had squared his shoulders and stared at nothing for a moment, Ogden said, " Listen outside any house in any street long enough and you'll hear the sound of people quarrelling. Nearly always it's the same two people in every family—husband and wife."

" Does that apply to your neighbours, Mr. and Mrs. Mitchell ? "

" Since they came to live here they've been no exception. The dividing wall between these two houses isn't very thick. If you raise your voice the people next door can hear almost every word."

" What did you hear ? "

" Just—quarrelling. He would say she didn't care tuppence if he dropped dead to-morrow so long as she was left well provided for. And she'd tell him that, if he felt that way, why didn't he get out ? Then he'd ask her what she thought she'd live on. She'd say if he left her he'd have to make her an allowance. . . ."

With a tight little grin that showed his teeth, Ogden shrugged. "If you're married men you'll know the kind of thing I'm talking about. Not that it means for one moment that she beat him over the head with a stick the other night."

Superintendent Mullett said, "When I spoke to Mrs. Mitchell a little while ago she told me you once threatened to beat the dog's head in if you ever caught it in your garden again."

In a flat voice, Ogden said, "Oh, she did, did she? Well, she's wrong. I didn't say that at all."

"What did you say?"

"I said I'd kick its teeth in," Ogden said. His eyes were a hard bright blue and his face was devoid of humour. "As it happens I'm quite fond of dogs, although I insist there are good ones and bad ones, clever ones and stupid ones, just like in people. It's the stupid, inconsiderate dog-worshipper that I don't like."

Mullett glanced at Sergeant Pugh and nodded. Pugh cleared his throat and said, "You mentioned someone else, sir, that Mr. Mitchell had quarrelled with. Who was that?"

Ogden looked at him with a theatrical air of surprise. "I'd just come to the conclusion that your job was to operate a concealed tape recorder so that anything I said could be taken down, twisted, and then used as evidence against me."

Pugh said, "I don't think the Superintendent will mind if I tell you, sir, that tape-recorded conversations are not admissible in an English court of law. And the phrase you've just misquoted should be: '. . . anything you say will be taken down in writing and may be used in evidence.'"

"Thank you, Sergeant. We're never too old to learn. Now, what was it you wanted to know . . . or doesn't it matter any longer? Incidentally, a lot of the things that policemen are made to say and do on television must annoy you."

In a mild voice, Superintendent Mullett said, "While people are watching television they aren't out committing the offences that keep Sergeant Pugh and me so busy—including the kind of offence that took place on the river bank the other night."

"Quite a thought, Superintendent. As it happens"—with wide eyes he looked up into Mullett's face and coughed—"I was watching TV that night."

"Were you alone, sir?"

"Well, my wife was in the house. She'd felt tired so she had gone to bed early. In one sense"—he shrugged again—"I suppose you could say I was alone."

"Did you leave home at all during the course of the evening—say, about half past ten or so?"

"No, I never stirred out . . . except to take a breath of fresh air at the gate. May I ask the reason for that question or"—his face was suddenly that of a bitter little man who thought he knew his rights—"should I know the answer?"

"I just thought you might've seen Mitchell setting out on his evening walk," Mullett said. "There was the possibility you might've noticed someone following him . . . that was all."

Ogden said, "I'm afraid I can't help you in that direction . . . but I can tell you the name of the other person he had a quarrel with."

"Who was that?"

"His brother-in-law, Mrs. Mitchell's brother. I believe his name's Newton, Jim Newton."

"What did they quarrel about?"

"I think it was over the way Mitchell treated his wife. I know there was a lot of shouting one evening about two or three weeks ago."

"Did Mrs. Mitchell take any part in this quarrel?"

"Not very much. I only heard her voice once or twice. The first time, she said: 'That's enough. . . .' Later I heard her say something like '. . . It's none of your business. . . .'"

"You couldn't tell, of course, whether she was speaking to her husband or her brother, could you?"

"No . . . and believe it or not, I wasn't very much interested." He jingled some keys in his pocket and let the sharp lines in his face smooth out. " Neither my wife nor I are the kind of people who get any fun out of the brawling of neighbours. We're not used to it. The folks who used to live next-door were a quiet elderly couple. We never heard a sound from Number 9 . . . until the Mitchells came to live here."

Mullett thought about the things Frank Mitchell's widow had told him, the emotionless way she had explained that her husband had not been of a quarrelsome disposition. There had been no guile in her meek voice when she said, ". . . *He isn't the kind to make enemies. We've been married nearly fifteen years and I've seldom known him to have words with anyone.*"

The Superintendent said, " Mrs. Mitchell gave me to understand they were quiet-living people, that her husband had no enemies even if he didn't have many friends. According to her he was the gentle, retiring type. What you say, Mr. Ogden, doesn't tally with that description, does it ? "

" What I say is the truth, nevertheless," Ogden said. He looked sincere and he sounded sincere.

If he were lying, the Superintendent told himself, he was a very convincing liar. Mullett said, " I wonder why she chose to give me a false impression."

" Why need it have been false at all ? Ordinarily, Mitchell was a quiet sort of chap. Even when I played hell with him about the way his dog had made a mess of my garden, he didn't really say anything to get my back up. He just promised he'd do his best to see it didn't happen again. It's his missus who can be the nasty type when she likes . . . if you want my opinion."

" Have you had any experience to justify that opinion ? "

" She was the one I spoke to the first time I complained about the non-stop yapping of that dog of theirs every time they went out and left it alone. Know what she said ? " His face hardened again. Without waiting for an answer, he went on, " She told me I was making a fuss over nothing . . . and in any case she could do as she liked in her own house."

" In other words, any unpleasantness you had was with her—not her husband ? "

" Well, that was all the satisfaction I got when I asked her in a very civil way if she would do something about the endless barking."

" So you feel that the female of the species was more deadly than the male . . . eh ? "

" It's generally the case, isn't it ? And it certainly applied to the Mitchells. I don't think he was a bad sort of chap at all. The fact that he answered back when his missus and her brother set about him doesn't mean a thing. Even the best-natured people are known to quarrel with their relations, aren't they ? "

" That's a thought worth bearing in mind," Superintendent Mullett said. He smoothed the front of his jacket, pondered for a moment, and then gave Ogden a little nod. " Thank you very much, sir, for being so patient with me. We won't take up any more of your time. . . ."

Sergeant Pugh lead the way to the front door. They went out on to the sunlit porch.

There Mullett turned and asked, " By the way, did your wife hear the sound of quarrelling from next door that you've described ? "

Ogden said, " No . . . at least, I don't think so." With no trace of impatience in his voice, he explained, " You see, she's out a lot. Belongs to a number of women's organisations and that kind of thing. I'm the stay-at-home in our family. I read, watch TV now and again, and in the summer I spend most of my time in the garden."

" Are you retired from business, Mr. Ogden ? I mean, we hardly expected to find you at home in the middle of a weekday morning."

" Oh, that . . ." He smiled easily and still seemed in no way anxious to see them go. " I'm on holiday right now. Wife's not been keeping too well so we didn't go away."

" Which means I'll be able to get in touch with you here during the next day or two if I think of anything I'd like to ask you ? "

" Yes, indeed. Any time, any time at all."

" Thank you again," Mullett said. " You've been most helpful. . . . Oh, just one thing more. Have you seen or heard anything of Mrs. Mitchell's brother—the fellow Newton you talked about—since he had a row with Mr. Mitchell two or three weeks ago ?"

With a slight change in his manner, Ogden said, "Yes, I have. He called next door the other night. I was taking the air at my garden gate when I saw him come and go. He knocked a couple of times and got no reply so he went away."

"What time would that be ?"

"It must've been not far off eleven o'clock. I was surprised to see him arrive so late."

"Do you remember which night it was ?"

"The night Mitchell was drowned," Ogden said. There was no emphasis in his voice, nothing in his face to indicate that he drew any conclusions from what he had just said.

The Superintendent murmured, "I see. . . . Much obliged to you, Mr. Ogden, for the information. Now, we'll let you get back to your work in the garden. Lovely weather we're having at the moment, isn't it ?"

"We could do with a drop of rain soon," Ogden said. "Good-bye."

He remained at the open door while Mullett and Sergeant Pugh walked to the gate and went out on to the pavement. He was still standing in the doorway as they climbed into the waiting car and drove off.

When the house was out of sight, Pugh said, "Wonder what explanation Newton will have for the visit he made here that night ?"

Superintendent Mullett said, "I'm more interested in where he went after he left here, and if he's the owner of a pair of grey flannel trousers with a piece ripped out of them. . . ."

They got back to Scotland Yard shortly before noon. It was about this time that Mrs. Alice Mitchell called on a solicitor by the name of Wheatley and instructed him to undertake the settlement of her late husband's estate.

CHAPTER VI

Early that afternoon the station inspector at Crown Road police station, Richmond, received a visitor who laid certain information before him. Subsequent to the interview he sent a written report by special messenger to Detective-Superintendent Mullett.

Following his brief preliminary remarks the inspector wrote:

. . . Although the complainant is known in the neighbourhood as something of an eccentric, I feel that the present investigation into the murder of Frank Albert Mitchell warrants my drawing your attention to the incident described by this person.

Her name is Edith Coupland, she is fifty-two years of age, and is a widow living alone in one of a block of converted flats at No. 16a Ham Street, Petersham. She states that she is of independent means, being in receipt of an income from investments left to her by her late husband.

At approximately 11.15 p.m. on the night of the attack on Frank Albert Mitchell, she claims that she was walking along the towpath on the south bank of the Thames almost opposite Marble Hill Park when she was accosted by a man who sprang upon her suddenly " . . . out of nowhere," to quote her own words. She is unable to describe this man, except that he had staring eyes and seemed to be panting for breath.

No attempt appears to have been made by him to commit any assault upon her. According to her statement he knocked her down apparently by accident and ran off in the darkness. She showed me a bruised elbow and a graze on the palm of her hand that she sustained when she fell.

I asked her why it had taken her so long to report

the occurrence. She said she had been afraid to do so in case her name got into the papers and the man took revenge on her for betraying him to the police. She had only come forward on the advice of a neighbour.

It should be borne in mind that Mrs. Coupland is obviously of a highly strung nature and, in the writer's opinion, has an over-developed imagination. Whatever it was that caused her to fall when she was walking along the towpath, it might well be that the story that she was attacked has its foundation in the account she read in her newspaper of the affair which occurred on the opposite bank of the river that same night.

I was unable to obtain from her any other details to support her statement. She admitted she was not in the habit of walking alone on the towpath at such a late hour. She had done so on that night because she had thought it might help her to sleep.

Mullett rang for Sergeant Pugh. As he handed him the report, he said, " Variation on an old theme. Any time now we should be having the usual bunch of psychopaths all insisting '. . . I done it.' What do you find so amusing, Sergeant ? "

Pugh said, " Bermondsey say a man walked in at nine o'clock this morning and confessed to the murder of Frank Mitchell. Seems Mitchell kidnapped his wife a couple of years ago and then did her in when he got tired of her. This fellow didn't catch up with him until the other night. When he did, the only thing to do was to kill him. . . . That's logical, isn't it, sir ? "

Superintendent Mullett said, " What the hell are you talking about, Sergeant ? "

" That's what he told the people at Bermondsey, sir. They checked his background and came up with a medical report. He's been a dip for years. Drinks anything that comes out of a bottle—except milk."

" And that business about his wife ? "

" Oh, she died four years ago. He's never got over it. When she went, he started drinking and forgot to stop. They say he's down to surgical spirit, now."

" You're a soulless devil," Mullett said. " I don't know how your wife puts up with you."

" Only because I pay the rent and support her children," Pugh said. " Did I tell you, sir, that I got in touch with British Railways and they managed to get hold of that fellow Newton's address ? "

" No, you didn't tell me. You were too busy being comical. I'd like a word with Mr. James Newton as soon as possible."

" You'll have to wait until late to-morrow afternoon, sir. He's not due back from Glasgow until then. His shift is working the dining car that left London at lunchtime to-day."

Mullett said, " Pity. But I suppose we can wait." He looked up at Pugh from under his brows and added, " One thing this job teaches a man, Sergeant, and that's patience."

Sergeant Pugh said, " Yes, sir. Anything you want me to do about this report from Richmond ? "

" Yes. When you've read it go and have a chat with Mrs. Edith Coupland."

James Newton returned to London late in the afternoon of July 13th. It was a hot, clammy day and the weather forecast said there was a likelihood of local thunderstorms.

Superintendent Mullett had been detained at a meeting with the deputy Commissioner so Sergeant Pugh conducted the interview in an office at Euston Station loaned for the purpose by the railway police. The room was small and dim and it had a sour smell of soot.

Newton took the line of vague indignation tinged with just the right amount of worry that could be expected of a man placed in his position. . . . Yes, he knew of his brother-in-law's death . . . read about it in a Glasgow evening paper. Yes, he'd phoned his sister soon as he heard the news and tried his best to comfort her. Promised he'd come straight to the house the minute he got back to town. If he was late, she'd get worried. After what had happened she needed someone around who was close to her. . . .

He was a male version of his sister : same small mouth and rather dull eyes, same kind of calm voice which used words without any inflexion. He had the same placid, submissive hands, too. It was difficult to imagine that either Mrs. Mitchell or her brother could ever raise their voices in anger.

Sergeant Pugh said, " If you don't want your sister to worry, why not give her a ring and tell her you're here talking to me ? Only take you a moment . . . and I don't mind waiting. Use the phone there."

" No . . . no, I don't think I really need to. You won't keep me long, will you ? " The only emotion he showed was a faint anxiety when he glanced at the clock on the wall. He was not disturbed by the idea of being questioned. If he had had any hand in the murder of his brother-in-law he had evidently no fear of being found out.

Pugh said, " According to statements made by two witnesses, Mr. Mitchell was attacked shortly after eleven o'clock on the night of July 9th. He must've left his home a little before eleven to take the dog for its usual evening walk, and we're trying to find someone who may have seen him on his way to the river bank."

With no understanding in his face, Newton said, " I see. . . ." The clock seemed to be his main interest.

" Where were you, Mr. Newton, about eleven o'clock that night ? "

" Me ? " He considered the question for a second or two with distant curiosity in his eyes. Then he asked, " Why do you want to know where I was ? "

" If you were anywhere near there that night you might've seen something of your brother-in-law."

Newton said, " Oh, I see what you mean." His little melancholy smile made him look more than ever like his sister. " I'm afraid I can't help you. The last time I saw Frank must've been two or three weeks ago."

" Please don't take offence if I repeat the question," Pugh said, " but I'd be obliged if you'd tell me where you were that night."

In a voice of pale indignation, Newton said, " Is that necessary ? "

" I wouldn't ask you otherwise," Pugh said.

" Probably not." He pondered for a moment and then sighed. " I'm sorry . . . but it's a bit difficult to remember."

" Please try, Mr. Newton."

" I'm trying. Let me see. . . . The ninth was. . . ."

" Last Sunday."

" Yes, of course. Well, I'm not sure but "—he made a little pointed mouth just like his sister's—" I believe I went to the pictures."

" Do you recall what you did or where you went after you came out of the pictures ? "

" No, I'm afraid I don't. It's five days ago." He looked at Pugh with regretful eyes. " I may have gone somewhere for a cup of coffee . . . or maybe I went straight back to my digs. I've a feeling I made an early night of it last Sunday."

Pugh said, " According to information we've received, you called at your sister's house that night at about eleven o'clock."

" Oh . . ." The look in his eyes had changed. He was no longer either curious or indignant. " Where did you get that information ? "

" From a man called Ogden. He says he saw you."

" Who's Ogden ? "

" Your sister's next-door neighbour."

When he had taken time for reflection, Newton said, " He's quite right. Now I remember. I did visit Richmond on Sunday night with the idea of seeing Alice. But I found no one at home."

" Wasn't it a bit late to go visiting, Mr. Newton ? "

" Not really. I had nothing better to do . . . and it was a nice night."

" Didn't you know your sister had gone to stay with friends for a few days and wouldn't be at home ? "

" No. If I had known I wouldn't have wasted my time going there. That's obvious, isn't it ? "

" Not necessarily. You might've wanted to keep your brother-in-law company for an hour while his wife was away."

" I might've done, but the point doesn't arise. I didn't know she was away."

A train rumbled into the station and pulled up with grinding brakes, the noisy gushing of a steam valve. From the platform just outside the office came the shrill blast of a whistle . . . doors slamming in broken sequence . . . footsteps slapping past at a run . . . the heavy panting of an engine . . . a voice calling "—see you next Wednesday. . . ."

Sergeant Pugh said, " Well, now we've got that settled, tell me, Mr. Newton: were you on reasonably close terms with Frank Mitchell ? "

The acrid tang of smoke seeped under the door. With breathless impatience the train began to move. As it gathered speed in the wake of a long thin howl from its whistle, Newton said, " I suppose you could say I was as close to him as the average man is to his sister's husband."

" What kind of man was he ? "

" Quiet. Never had much to say for himself. That's what makes it all so strange. . . ." Newton left the comment unfinished. He seemed sorry he had amplified his answer at all.

" Makes what so strange ? "

" That he of all people should go and get himself killed like this. He never carried much money and he certainly didn't look the type that would be worth robbing. Wore a cap and an old suit in the evening when he took the dog for a walk. Whoever did it couldn't have got much."

" You think robbery was the motive behind the attack on him ? "

" What other motive could there have been ? "

" That's what we're trying to find out," Pugh said.

Newton gave him a sidelong glance and then turned his head to look at the clock again. When he could no longer remain silent, he said, " There couldn't be any other motive. Frank couldn't have made anyone dislike him enough—to do a thing like that."

" Maybe dislike didn't enter into it. His wife says he had very few friends, incidentally. How did you get on with him ? "

" All right. As I've told you, he was a quiet sort of man. You couldn't either like him or dislike him to any great extent. Kind of negative . . . if you know what I mean. But he was good-hearted in his own way."

" You mean generous with money ? "

" Well, I suppose you could call it generous. Sometimes, in my opinion, he let people take liberties with him."

" In what way ? "

" Oh, he let them run up accounts and when they didn't pay he wouldn't go for them . . . because one of the kids was sick or the fellow's wife was going into hospital . . . or something like that." Newton's eyes left Pugh's face and flitted to the clock on the wall. " Silly . . . that's what I call it."

" Do you know if he ever had a row with anyone—either over money or anything else ? "

" Not as far as I'm aware."

" Did he ever tell you about some unpleasantness with the man next door because the dog barked a lot when your sister and her husband went out ? "

Newton made a small, pointed mouth again and shook his head. " No. This is the first I've heard of it." He seemed to be showing interest only because it was the polite thing to do.

" Then you'd say the trouble between him and the man next door couldn't have been very serious ? "

" I can only tell you that Frank wasn't the kind of man people quarrel with very easily."

" But you quarrelled with him," Pugh said.

For one brief moment Newton looked taken aback. Then he relaxed. In the placid voice that never altered, he said, " Who told you that Frank and I quarrelled ? "

" Ogden, the man who lives at Number 11 Douglas Crescent."

" Perhaps it's about time someone told this fellow Ogden to mind his own business."

" The death of your brother-in-law makes it our business," Pugh said. " Did you, in fact, have a row with Mitchell two or three weeks before he was killed ? "

" No. We never had a wrong word in all the years he

was married to my sister. I told him off a few times—not that it made any difference—but there was never any quarrel between us."

"Why did you tell him off?"

"Because he let people treat him as a mug."

"Over money they owed him?"

"Yes."

"Would it be on one of those occasions that the man next door heard loud voices engaged in what he thought was a quarrel?"

"Possibly. I don't see that it's of any importance, anyway."

"It might be. Do you recollect what your sister said that night?"

"No. What does the Nosey Parker next door say she said?"

"He says he heard her shout 'Mind your own business. . . .' Do you remember anything like that?"

Without expression, Newton said, "I don't think my sister's ever shouted in her life. If she raises her voice at all it's most unusual."

"All right, let's assume she raised her voice sufficiently for the man next-door to hear what she was saying. Do you recollect her using those words?"

"Vaguely, yes. If she did, she was talking to me."

"Why should she say that to you?"

"Oh, I'd lost my patience with Frank because he'd been soft with someone again. Cost him a good few pounds, too, if I remember rightly."

"Your only reason for being angry with him was because he wasn't hard enough with people who owed him money?"

"That's right . . . if you could call it being angry."

"And there was no other disagreement between you and your brother-in-law?"

"There was no disagreement at all. I just told him he was a mug, that was all. Now, I'd like you to tell me something."

"Yes?"

"Have you got some idea at the back of your mind that I had something to do with Frank's death?"

The question came out as though he had been awaiting a suitable opportunity to ask it. He was neither angry nor concerned. He just wanted to know.

Sergeant Pugh said, " Now you've put the thought in my mind, Mr. Newton. I wasn't suggesting any such thing. What motive would you have for killing him ? "

" None at all. But you can't forget that I might've had the opportunity. And it worries you, doesn't it ? That's the reason you were waiting for me when my train got in."

" We have to question everybody connected with Mr. Mitchell. But, since you ask me, you couldn't have been very far away from the spot at the time of his death . . . could you ? "

" I don't know what time that was," Newton said. He was still glancing at the clock like a man who was afraid he might be late for an appointment.

Pugh laid himself odds that James Newton would talk too much if he were given the right kind of encouragement. They always talked too much. Nine cases out of ten would never reach court if they kept their mouths shut. . . .

He said, " Two people who saw your brother-in-law drown, Mr. Newton, say that the time was a few minutes after eleven o'clock. If you had wanted you could have gone from your sister's house to that spot on the river bank where Mitchell was attacked and pushed into the water. You see that, don't you ? "

" If I had wanted," Newton said. He seemed to play with the idea before he added, " No one would suggest a thing like that unless they were also prepared to believe I was out of my mind. I'd have to be mad to kill my sister's husband for no reason at all."

" The man next door says he heard you quarrelling," Pugh said.

" I've already explained that it wasn't a quarrel. My sister will bear me out on that. She was there."

" Mrs. Mitchell could scarcely be considered unbiased."

Newton made a little gesture of impatience. He said, " Look here, Sergeant, I think this has gone far enough. I've been working all day and I'm beginning to feel tired. Let's cut out this suggestion business. If you've any further questions, please ask them so we can get it over and done with."

Sergeant Pugh said, " Very good, Mr. Newton. I'd be glad if you'd tell me where you were at eleven o'clock on the night of July the ninth."

Without the slightest hesitation, Newton said, " On a bus."

" Which bus ? "

" One I caught at the main road after I left Douglas Crescent. It took me to Richmond Station."

" And from there ? "

" I went home to my digs at King's Cross."

" How long did it take you ? "

" About an hour, give or take five minutes. I was lucky enough to catch a train almost right away . . . and I had only a couple of minutes to wait when I changed at Earl's Court to the Piccadilly Line."

" So you must've got home about midnight ? "

" Or just a few minutes after that. It couldn't have been much after twelve."

" Did you speak to anyone you knew on the way—or when you arrived home ? "

" Yes. I had a couple of words with a fellow who has a room across the passage from mine. If you don't believe me, Sergeant. . . ."

" Why should you think I don't believe you ? "

" I can tell by the look on your face. But the man I spoke to will probably remember it. If you want to confirm whether or not I'm telling the truth "—Newton's shrug was almost a feminine gesture—" I won't mind at all."

" The thought I had wasn't what you imagined," Pugh said. " I was just asking myself why you should suddenly remember the exact details of your journey and what happened on your arrival home, when only a few minutes ago you couldn't even remember that you'd been to Richmond that night."

The passing annoyance that came and went in Newton's smooth soft face reflected itself in his voice. He said, " That's near enough to calling me a liar, Sergeant."

" I was merely stating the facts, Mr. Newton." At the

back of Pugh's mind was the realisation that further questioning would produce nothing of value.

. . . *He wouldn't have given me this story if he wasn't sure it would be substantiated. . . . But the fact that he arrived home just after twelve on the night of Mitchell's death proves nothing either way. . . .*

It was no more than a few minutes walk from Douglas Crescent to the river bank. Knowing Mitchell's nightly itinerary, he could have reached the little clearing behind the bushes before Mitchell got there and then waited out of sight. The rest was only a matter of seconds in what could have been a carefully calculated time-table.

. . . *When the job was done he could've made his way to the main Richmond road and caught a bus only four or five minutes later than he would've done if he'd gone straight from his sister's address. Those few minutes are now safely swallowed up in the hour's journey from Richmond to King's Cross. . . .*

No proof . . . no motive. . . . He must've had a motive if he did plan and carry out deliberate murder. And why did he leave himself open to suspicion by calling at his sister's house at all that night? Why did he let himself be seen when there was no need? It looks almost as if he wanted someone to see him . . . unless, of course, his story is true. . . .

James Newton stood up and massaged his hands and looked at the clock again. He said, " I don't want to rush you, Sergeant, but I really must be off. I know you're only trying to do your job and, if it means anything to you, I hope you find the one who did it. I liked Frank and "—he shook his head and made a sad face that had no real feeling behind it—" I hope the person who killed him is caught and punished."

" We hope so, too," Pugh said.

Newton nodded. As he opened the door, he said, " I wish you luck. . . ." Then he went out into the noise and bustle of the busy platform without looking back. He left the door open.

Sergeant Pugh snapped a rubber band round his notebook and put his pen away. By the time he left the office there was no sign of James Newton.

In the sergeant's mind one thought remained to tease him. *I wouldn't trust you or your sister as far as I could throw either of you. But what motive could you have had? That clever character who lives next-door says you quarrelled. You say you didn't quarrel. Who's to prove whether you did or not?*

Even if Newton and Mitchell had had a row, weeks had elapsed before Mitchell was savagely attacked. There was not even a shred of evidence against anyone.

The way things stood, Newton had no motive . . . Ogden was hardly capable physically of taking Mitchell's stick away from him and using it with such deadly effect . . . and that left the man called Heald. . . . What kind of case could be made out against him, anyway?

Mullett's theory was ingenious, but it took more than theories to support a prosecution. *And that*, Sergeant Pugh said to himself, *brings us right back to where we started. Now I'd better go and have a chat with the woman who says she was assaulted the night somebody bashed Frank Albert Mitchell over the head with his own stick. Hope she's at home this time. . . .*

CHAPTER VII

MRS. EDITH COUPLAND could add little or nothing to the story she had told the inspector at Crown Road police station. In spite of her unwavering insistence that everything had happened just as she had described it, her manner hardly inspired confidence.

Before two minutes had elapsed Sergeant Pugh mentally classified her as the type that twittered. All the time she was speaking to him she fidgeted with one thing or another, touching her hair, fussing with the bracelet of her wristwatch, smoothing down her skirt as if she were afraid he might see more of her legs than was proper.

She was a small dark woman who had evidently used something on her hair to conceal the fact that she was going grey. At some time long ago she might have been superficially pretty, but the passing years had taken more than her youth. Somewhere along the way her nervous system had set about a process of self-destruction.

While Pugh sat and made notes, she walked agitatedly to and fro, talking too much and too fast, flapping her hands whenever she failed to find the right descriptive word. Nevertheless, her account of what she said had taken place differed in no material respect from what she had told the station inspector.

. . . Maybe the man had not really had staring eyes . . . but he was certainly breathing very hard as if he had run a long way. . . .

" No, I didn't see where he came from. Jumped out at me without any warning. I don't know how I didn't die there and then. I'm not right yet, I can assure you. Whenever I do manage to get to sleep I have terrible dreams. After all, an experience like that is bound to leave its mark. . . ."

Sergeant Pugh said, " Yes, madam," or " No, madam," according to the tone of her voice. Long before the interview was over he had made up his mind that she had imagined the whole thing. Super's orders had to be obeyed to the letter, but this trip out to Richmond was nothing more nor less than a waste of time.

Even if she were not a neurotic there was nothing of value in what she had to say. The incident, after all, had occurred on the opposite bank of the river. Except that the time was the same, there was no reason to believe the two events were in any way related.

" If you didn't see where this man came from, Mrs. Coupland, have you any idea which direction he took after he knocked you down ? "

" No, I'm afraid I can't tell you that, either. You see, it was dark and I was terribly shaken, as you can well imagine, and by the time I picked myself up again I was feeling more dead than alive and I don't think I even knew where I was, far less keep track of where that ruffian had gone. The only thing I hoped and prayed was that he had gone. . . ."

" Yes, madam."

"How I managed to get home that night I'll never know. Every minute I thought I was going to faint. When at last I got indoors, well, I just collapsed and I don't remember any more. . . ."

Mrs. Edith Coupland went on talking. Sergeant Pugh stopped pretending to make notes after a while but it made no difference.

Finally, he got away. As he took his leave of her, she was once again telling him it was a wonder she had not died.

The Misses Ward were a different type: quiet gentle people who lived in a house that had the atmosphere of a museum, the air of a place in which no voices were ever raised, no emotions ever allowed to step beyond the bounds of propriety.

There was an illuminated text hanging in the hall: *The Meek Shall Inherit the Earth.* A leather-bound Bible lay on the table in the room where they received Detective-Sergeant Pugh.

The furniture belonged to a by-gone generation and the photographs on the sideboard were of people dressed in the style of men and women who must have died a long, long time ago. On the mantelpiece stood a gilt and marble clock with a sonorous tick that took Pugh's mind back to the days when he was very young.

Miss Margaret spoke for both her sister and herself. Miss Mary had very little to say.

. . . Yes, a great tragedy, a great tragedy indeed. . . . Men did such wicked deeds these days. . . . The Lord giveth and the Lord taketh away . . . poor, dear Alice. Such a sweet girl to be so sorely afflicted. . . . A policeman must see many dreadful things in his daily work. . . .

Pugh said, "I'm afraid I do. Are you on the telephone, Miss Margaret?"

"No, we aren't . . . I'm sorry. But if you wanted to make a call there's a box at the corner of the street. You turn left when you leave here, and then left again and—"

"It wasn't that," Pugh said. "I just wondered if Mr. Mitchell might've tried to get in touch with his wife that Sunday night."

" Oh . . ." The sisters looked at each other. Then Miss Margaret asked, " Why should he have wanted to do that ? "

" No reason that I know of . . . merely a passing thought, that was all. As you will appreciate, we're working very much in the dark."

Miss Margaret stroked one hand over the other while she meditated. At last, she said, " If we did possess a phone—which we don't—poor Mr. Mitchell wouldn't have been able to speak to his wife during the early evening, anyway."

Sergeant Pugh felt a slight stirring of interest for the first time since he had entered the house. He said, " Why ? Had she gone out ? "

In a tone of mild correction, Miss Margaret said, " All three of us had gone out. We attended evening service. My sister and I always do and, when Alice Mitchell comes to stay with us, we take her along—naturally."

" Naturally," Pugh said. His interest had evaporated. " Did you come straight back here from church ? "

" Oh, yes. We're always home again by half past nine. Unlike so many gadabout people nowadays, we keep early hours in this family." The Misses Ward looked at each other again with mutual satisfaction.

Pugh said, " Most nights I wish I had the chance to be in bed by ten o'clock. I consider that's late enough, but my family have different ideas."

" We do better than that on the Sabbath. I can't remember a Sunday night when we haven't retired by, at the very latest, a quarter to ten. Can you, Mary ? "

Miss Mary was unable to remember any exception to their regular practice. With what she seemed to regard as a touch of daring, she added, " If Frank Mitchell hadn't been out-of-doors at an hour when he should've been in bed, he might well be alive to-day."

Her sister nodded gravely. " To be sure. . . . But we mustn't question the ways of the Lord. Was there anything else you wanted to ask us, Sergeant ? "

" No, thank you. And I must be getting along, now. . . ."

Both of them saw him to the door. He knew they were watching him from behind the front-room curtains as he walked to the gate.

. . . Two prematurely-aged spinsters whose lives were wrapped around Sunday church service and an occasional visit from Mrs. Alice Mitchell . . . they badly lacked friends if Mrs. Mitchell was the best they could find to entertain. Of course, she was quiet and reserved like they were themselves . . . probably they got along together very well. . . .

His thoughts shifted. He wondered what the Misses Ward would say if they even suspected the idea he was nursing in his head right then.

. . . Supposing Mrs. Mitchell owned a car or had hired a car ? Supposing she had left the two sisters sound asleep in bed that night and had driven from Catford to Richmond ? How long would the journey have taken her if traffic was not heavy ?

Could she have reached that spot on the banks of the Thames near Marble Hill Park before her husband passed there on his nightly walk ? And if so . . . why should she have wanted to kill him ?

CHAPTER VIII

It rained heavily over the week-end. Superintendent Mullett spent most of the time in his office, clearing up arrears of routine work, checking any and every report that appeared to have even the slightest bearing on the murder of Frank Albert Mitchell.

Occasionally he passed some thoughtful minutes looking out of his window at the rain-scoured Embankment where the swollen waters of the Thames surged between the piers of Westminster Bridge. He did a lot of thinking during Saturday and Sunday.

If and when they recovered Mitchell's body it would assist the investigation very little, if at all. They already knew he had been brutally beaten about the head with his own stick before he entered the water. Whether he had died from those injuries or from drowning was immaterial. Either way, he had been the victim of murder.

The results of the interviews that Sergeant Pugh had conducted on Friday were interesting but not very informative, except that Mrs. Mitchell now had no real alibi for the time of her husband's death. Mrs. Edith Coupland's story about the alleged assault on the south bank of the river was no more credible at the second telling than it had been at the first. Even if it were true, she was unable to furnish a description of her assailant.

. . . Of course, it was just possible that she was not imagining the whole thing. She might have been knocked down by the man who had killed Mitchell. . . .

Mullett asked himself if they were up against one of those maniac cases. But if the man was a maniac why had he not killed Mrs. Coupland, too ? Anyway, the two events had occurred on different sides of the river. It was all very trying.

All he could do was go on sifting the bits and pieces of information that came his way in the hope that something might turn up. Now, if Ogden or Heald or James Newton owned a pair of grey flannels and those grey flannels had a piece torn out of them—that would be something.

But search warrants were not issued without evidence that they were justified. And there was no evidence, no evidence at all. When the killer fled into the darkness that night he had vanished without trace.

At that point, Superintendent Mullett stopped doodling on his memo pad and wrote : *He—or she.* Mrs. Alice Mitchell might behave like a stupid woman, but appearances could be deceptive.

If only something indicated the existence of another man . . . that would be motive all right. Many a woman had disposed of an unwanted husband—or she had provided the evil inspiration for her lover to do so.

The Superintendent went home on Sunday evening in a very dissatisfied frame of mind. He had an uncomfortable feeling that this might well prove to be one of those cases where the police believed they knew the answer but were never able to prove it.

On Monday morning, July 17th, he had scarcely started work when he was told that someone wished to see him in connection with the case of Frank Albert Mitchell. The visitor was a Mr. John Piper, an insurance assessor acting for the Cresset Insurance Company.

Mullett said, " Send him up . . . and see if you can find Sergeant Pugh for me."

Pugh was somewhere in the building. The switchboard said they would get hold of him as soon as they could. Then Piper was ushered into the superintendent's office.

When he had asked him to take a seat and offered him a cigarette, Mullett said, " I've heard of you, Mr. Piper. Worked with one or two of our people before, haven't you ? "

Piper said, " Yes. I know several of the officers here quite well, particularly Detective-Inspector Hoyle."

" It was Hoyle who mentioned your name not so long ago. He has a pretty good opinion of you, Mr. Piper."

" I'm glad to hear it . . . especially since we haven't always seen eye to eye on some things."

" Differences of view point don't matter," Mullett said. " What is important to a policeman is that you're on his side of the fence. Now "—he leaned back and folded his arms—" what is this information you have about the Mitchell affair ? "

" A solicitor called Wheatley got in touch with the Cresset Insurance Company first thing this morning," Piper said. " He told them he was acting on behalf of a Mrs. Alice Mitchell. It appears that Mrs. Mitchell has instructed him to apply for probate of her late husband's will."

Superintendent Mullett said, " Oh, she has, has she ? The lady doesn't seem to believe in wasting time. Ever read the Bible, Mr. Piper ? "

" Not very often, I'm afraid."

" I don't, either. But I remember a line from the Book of Proverbs which I hope for the lady's sake doesn't apply to her actions: *He that maketh haste to be rich shall not be innocent. . . .*"

"That was very much the thought which struck me," Piper said. "In a case of natural death, the widow's behaviour need be governed by nothing more than her own ideas of what is, or what is not, conventional. But murder puts things in a very different light."

The superintendent said, "How right you are. . . . What was her solicitor after?"

"The nature of the insurance policy the late Mr. Mitchell had held."

"Didn't his wife know?"

"Apparently she was aware that he carried life assurance with the Cresset, but she didn't know the details."

"M-m-m. . . . That is interesting. Who's holding the policy?"

"Wheatley says she hasn't got it and neither has he. They've checked with the bank and it isn't there, either."

"Sounds as if the late Mr. Mitchell was either very careless—or very careful. Was Wheatley his solicitor, too?"

"Yes. Handled all his business."

"But wasn't trusted with the safe-keeping of the policy. How long ago did Mitchell take out his insurance with the Cresset?"

"About twelve years ago."

"For how much?"

"Ten thousand pounds," Piper said.

Mullett rubbed his chin and looked at him quizzically. "You don't say!" Then he unfolded his arms and eased himself upright and gave Piper a small grin. "Well, well, well! If I tell you something, you'll keep it confidential, of course?"

Piper said, "Of course. Whatever you say at any time will go no further."

"Good. Firstly, I've been rather curious about Mrs. Alice Mitchell and her brother, a bloke called Newton. Mrs. Mitchell was away from home the night her husband got himself killed, but Newton says he didn't know this and visited the house with the idea of seeing her. He found no one at home. We've had that confirmed by the next-door neighbour."

"What time would that be?"

"Near enough the time Frank Mitchell copped a packet on the river bank."

"Awkward for Mr. Newton—in the circumstances."

"Could be. I've been wondering if brother or sister might've had a financial motive, but I didn't think it would be ten thousand pounds' worth."

"Motive isn't everything," Piper said, "even if one or both of them had the opportunity. Do you think they had anything to do with it?"

Superintendent Mullett said, "I don't know. If they did, and we can prove it, the Cresset'll save themselves a lot of money, won't they?"

"No company objects to paying out claims. In fact, they like it . . . so long as the claims are legitimate. If a woman murders her husband, or is guilty of complicity in the murder of her husband—that's different. She isn't entitled by law to benefit from the commission of a felony . . . if you don't mind my quoting law to you."

"Not in the least. You can quote anything you like—except Shakespeare." Mullett drew a ring around Mrs. Mitchell's name on his memo pad and laid his pencil on the desk. "In this office I use all the Shakespearian quotations. They serve to lay a veneer of wisdom over a not very wise policeman's remarks."

There was a quick double knock at the door and Sergeant Pugh poked his head in. He said, "I believe you wanted me, sir?"

"Yes, I did. Come in and shut the door. . . . This is Mr. Piper who represents the Cresset Insurance Company in re the affairs of the late Frank Albert Mitchell. . . . I'd like you to meet Detective-Sergeant Pugh, Mr. Piper. He's working on this case with me. I think he'll be more than interested in the news you've just brought. Would you mind repeating what you told me? . . ."

Pugh took a chair and listened. He had heard of this John Piper, but it was the first time they had ever met.

. . . *Big fellow with a good appearance. . . . Looks more*

like a copper than the average copper does. Wears good clothes . . . must be earning more than a copper's wages. . . .

When they had talked for a little while, Piper said, " I'd like to be of help, Superintendent, if that isn't an impertinence coming from an outsider."

" No policeman thinks anyone's impertinent who offers his help," Mullett said. " When I'm up against a case of murder I don't mind forming a mutual-aid society. Still, what do you think you can do that we can't ? "

" I'm a private citizen, not a policeman. Sometimes that can be an advantage. If I behave indiscreetly I don't lose my job."

" True. What do you think, Sergeant ? "

Sergeant Pugh said, " Can't do much harm, sir, so long as Mr. Piper isn't too indiscreet. And I've got a feeling, anyway. . . ."

" Your feelings always depress me, Sergeant. What is it this time ? "

" I've come to the conclusion that it's not going to be easy to pin this thing on Mrs. Mitchell and her brother, sir. They may have had all the motive and opportunity in the world, but there isn't a shred of real evidence against either of them."

Superintendent Mullett said, " If they did it, we'll get 'em." Then he grinned at Piper and added, "—I hope."

CHAPTER IX

THE BRISK little man busily clipping the hedge outside Number 11 Douglas Crescent glanced over his shoulder as Piper went by. Very politely, he said, " Good morning. Lovely day after the rain, isn't it ? "

Piper said, " Very pleasant, indeed."

He wondered if Mrs. Mitchell's neighbour greeted every stranger who passed by while he was working outside his house. . . . This must be the man called Ogden. The Superintendent had described him well. Hardly looked the type who indulged in unnecessary courtesies.

. . . What was it Superintendent Mullett had called him . . . ? Yes, aggressive was the right word. The Americans had an apt phrase for it : a chip on his shoulder. . . .

Yet, Ogden looked contented enough as he worked in the mid-morning sunshine with his sleeves rolled up. His face and his muscular arms were tanned and glistening with sweat.

Gardening evidently kept him in good condition. There seemed no physical reason why it could not have been one of those hard, capable hands that had wrested the walking-stick from Frank Mitchell and used it viciously on both Mitchell and his dog.

Not a very civilised act, perhaps, by someone who enjoyed a gentle hobby like gardening. . . . But Mullett had quoted something that he said had been written more than three hundred years ago by Dryden : *Beware the fury of a patient man.*

How patient had Mitchell's neighbour been ? How long had he perhaps waited until the opportunity presented itself ?

There was no reply from number 9. Piper touched the bell-push again and listened to the bell ringing sharply. The third time he kept his finger on the button for several seconds. Then he went down the path to the gate.

The little man had laid aside his shears and was energetically sweeping the pavement. Just outside his own gate he had collected a mound of hedge clippings.

Piper said, " Excuse me. . . . Mrs. Mitchell appears to be out. Have you any idea when she'll be back ? "

While he felt in a trouser pocket for a handkerchief the little man leaned on his brush. He wiped his face and then said, " I heard the bath water running out not many minutes ago . . . so she must still be in the house. Probably she couldn't answer the door because she's getting dressed. I advise you to wait a couple of minutes and then try again."

" Thank you," Piper said. " I'll do that."

Ogden finished with his handkerchief and put it away. With his eyes fixed on Piper's face, he asked, " Are you another policeman ? "

" No. I suppose you've had quite a few round here recently ? "

" Well, two detectives called on me the other day. One was a big noise from Scotland Yard. I thought you might be one of his men."

" My job is much less exciting than that," Piper said.

The look of interest faded from Ogden's hard blue eyes. He said, " Well, I suppose I should be getting on with my work. I've got quite a bit to do before lunchtime. Try next door now. You might have more luck this time. . . ."

Inside number 9 there were sounds of someone moving about. Piper took off his hat and touched the bell-push lightly once.

He heard footsteps coming down the stairs—careful, unhurried footsteps that stopped when they reached the hall as though she were waiting for him to ring again. With the sun behind him he knew she must be able to see his silhouette through the glass panels of the door.

. . . *Perhaps she's got the same impression as the fellow at number* 11 . . . *perhaps she isn't over-anxious to talk to another policeman. . . . Wonder what she's like, this woman who inherited a fortune the night her husband lost his life in the Thames ?* . . .

As if in answer to the question in his mind, the door opened. Piper said, " Good morning. Mrs. Mitchell ? "

" Yes. What is it you want ? "

In that first moment he knew why Superintendent Mullett had found it so difficult to describe her. She had characterless features, mousy hair and placid eyes that were not those of an intelligent woman.

Piper said, " I've been asked by the Cresset Insurance Company to call and have a chat with you, Mrs. Mitchell. May I come in ? "

With no change of expression in her pale plump face, she said, " Yes . . . you can if you want to. I didn't think. . . ." He was left to complete the missing words for himself.

She led him into a dull cold room furnished with a circular table, a big oak chest under the window, and a sideboard against the opposite wall. Four chairs were grouped at equal distances around the table in the centre of which stood a wilting hydrangea.

A variety of ornaments decorated the oak mantleshelf: three china elephants in a line, trunk linked to tail; a carved wooden dog; two plates painted in colour with pictures of what looked like parakeets perched on a branch; a small vase in brown unglazed pottery coarsely daubed with a representation of biblical characters picking figs.

There was a mahogany clock with a silver dial on the lower shelf. It had stopped.

The blue-and-fawn carpet square was not big enough to cover the entire floor space. At each end of the room there were rectangles of linoleum in a parquetry design.

Mrs. Mitchell remained standing. She said, " What is it you want to talk to me about ? "

" A man called Wheatley phoned the Cresset Insurance Company this morning. He says he's your solicitor."

As if Piper had asked a question, Mrs. Mitchell said, " Yes, Mr. Wheatley is my solicitor. He's taking care of my husband's estate . . . and things like that."

" It seems he's been unable to trace your late husband's life insurance policy. From what I've been told no one knows where it is."

" Yes . . . it's quite true. We've searched everywhere

. . . and asked at the bank . . . but we can't find it." She was only mildly disturbed.

" Was Mr. Mitchell normally a methodical person ? "

" Oh, yes. That's what makes it so . . ." She left Piper to finish the sentence and stared down at the polished top of the table as though studying her blurred reflection.

" Do you remember when you last saw the policy ? "

" I don't think I've ever seen it. In fact "—she made a little circle on the table with her forefinger and then glanced at him—" I'm sure I haven't."

" Didn't he ever discuss that kind of thing with you ? "

" No. There was never any need. He looked after all business matters . . . like that."

" Didn't you talk it over when he first proposed taking out a policy ? "

" Neither then nor at any time since."

" Rather an unusual situation," Piper said. " How did you get to know his life had been insured with the Cresset ? "

" Oh, that was quite simple. You see "—Mrs. Mitchell's soft patient voice became even more patient—" I had a conversation on Saturday morning with the bank manager. We had to make some arrangements about the account so as to keep the shop going until the estate is settled. You know how complicated these things are."

" You intend to carry on your husband's business ? "

" Only for the time being. Mr. Wheatley is going to find someone to buy it from me." With the air of taking him into her confidence, Mrs. Mitchell added, " You see, it's never been what you could really call a prosperous business. Anyway, I wouldn't be much good. . . ." She drew another little circle on the table top while she looked at Piper absently.

He said, " It's always very difficult for a woman in your position, Mrs. Mitchell, I'm afraid. What was it you found out about your husband's insurance when you called at the bank ? "

" The manager and I had to go through some papers and he explained to me that Frank always left him to pay things like rates and mortgage repayments and so on whenever they became due. . . ." She looked at the tip of her forefinger and then rubbed finger and thumb together. " You know the way banks look after that sort of thing, don't you ? "

" Yes, I know," Piper said.

He was asking himself if the superintendent had not been right. Without much doubt, Mrs. Mitchell was a stupid woman. Her explanations were those of a slow-thinking person. On the other hand, they could be intended to convey that impression deliberately. . . .

Alice Mitchell said, " The manager told me he had a standing order to pay the Cresset Insurance Company the annual premiums on a policy. The bank had been paying them for a number of years. Of course they would stop now because. . . ." Her eyes told Piper she was thinking of her husband. Whatever her thoughts were they caused her no distress.

" So Saturday was the first time you became aware that your husband was insured ? "

" Yes. I'd never given that sort of thing any thought. Of course, after he—died . . ." Her small hushed voice trailed away into silence.

Piper said, " It's a great pity you're unable to find the policy. No company likes the idea of issuing copies. They always urge policy holders to make sure the document is kept in a safe place, mainly because it's awkward for the widow, for example, in a situation like this."

Mrs. Mitchell said, " Yes, of course . . ." Judging by her tone her mind was on something else.

" Didn't Mr. Wheatley advise you that the insurance company is entitled to insist on production of the policy ? "

With an obvious effort, she concentrated on the question. At last, she said, " No. I only spent a few minutes with him. He told me to leave everything in his hands. If I did come across the policy I was to let him know."

" Did he mention that the company will also have to be furnished with a death certificate ? "

" Oh, will they ? " She seemed only mildly surprised.

" I'm afraid so. They must have documented proof of death. In this case, so far as I'm aware, there's been no inquest yet."

" But surely someone must be able to issue a certificate ? " Her eyes were beginning to look worried. Piper told himself he had found the first chink in her shell of composure.

. . . *This may be the weak link we've been looking for. Frank Mitchell wasn't meant to drown. Mullett's suggestion was probably pretty near the mark. Mitchell must've fallen into the river when he was trying to escape . . . the job was badly handled in that case. He should've been found dead beside the body of his dog. . . .*

Piper said, " You may have to apply to the High Court for leave to presume the death of your husband. But, of course, your solicitor is the man to advise you on that matter."

She looked at him as though he were personally responsible for her unexpected problem. Then she asked, " How long would that take ? "

" In the ordinary way, when a man disappears and can't be traced, the court won't grant presumption of death until seven years have elapsed. The circumstances in this case are somewhat different, of course."

" They certainly are," Mrs. Mitchell said. She walked to the window, turned slowly, and clasped her hands in front of her. With annoyance sharpening her quiet voice, she said, " You're in the insurance business. You must've come across similar things before. How long would you say it'll take in this case ? "

" I don't really know," Piper said. " Maybe six months, maybe more. I doubt if anyone could tell you definitely. It all depends on the length of time the court considers proper."

" But the policeman I spoke to talked about two people seeing Frank drown. If he's drowned he's dead . . . and I've lost my husband. What am I supposed to live on while some court makes up its mind whether I'm a widow or not ? "

" It isn't my fault," Piper said.

" No . . . no, of course not. But it all seems very silly to me. While I'm kept waiting like this I can't sell the shop . . . or anything. That's apart from getting my money from the insurance company. If they gave me that it wouldn't be so bad." Vexation came into her plump, empty face. " You say they won't do that . . . will they ? "

" Not without a death certificate. Insurance officials always want a piece of paper. In this case there's a question of a lost policy as well."

She stared through him as though she found it difficult to absorb what he was saying. In an absent voice, she murmured, " I just don't know what to do. He was a good husband . . . and he paid the premiums for years so that I'd be provided for if anything happened to him. Now it has happened. . . ."

Little bitter lines formed at the corners of her mouth. Without much interest, she asked, " How much was he insured for, anyway ? "

" Ten thousand pounds," Piper said.

Her mouth opened and her hands slid apart. She took a deep breath before she managed to say, " You must be mistaken. Frank couldn't afford as much as that. . . ."

" No, that's the figure he insured his life for. There's no mistake."

" I can't believe it. He never even told me . . ." The fingers of one hand plucked at her dark dress while she went on staring at Piper as if she still doubted his word. " Are you sure you aren't getting my husband's policy mixed up with—somebody else's ? "

" Quite sure."

Mrs. Mitchell felt for a chair and sat down and put both hands to her face. When she had taken another long breath, she said, " Oh, dear . . . oh, dear. . . . All these years, and I never knew he thought as much of me as that. Why didn't he say ? Why did he have to keep it a secret ? Poor Frank . . . all these years. . . ."

" Most men know their wives don't like to discuss life insurance," Piper told her. " The important thing right now is to find out where he put the policy. Do please make another search among his papers in case you've overlooked it."

" Yes . . . yes, I will. But surely it won't matter so

very much even if we don't find it? After all, he never missed paying any of the premiums . . . and the insurance company must keep records. It's not as if . . ." She was afraid to complete the thought.

"The company must take into account the possibility that your husband may have used his policy as security for a loan. While that possibility exists they obviously can't pay you the total sum assured even if you get probate of his will fairly quickly. They must first be satisfied that no one has a charge on the policy. You understand that, don't you?"

"Well, I—I think so." Her composure was returning. Beyond question she had had a shock. Some of its effects still lingered.

Piper's thoughts now led to only one conclusion. Superintendent Mullett had picked on the wrong motive.

. . . *The fact that Frank Mitchell was insured for a substantial sum of money can't have had anything to do with it. If his wife didn't know how much he was insured for, then neither did her brother. It might've been for fifty . . . or a hundred pounds. . . .*

They wouldn't resort to murder unless they knew how much they were going to get out of it. And she didn't until I told her. . . . Supposing neither she nor her brother had anything to do with it? Maybe it was that fellow Heald . . . or somebody else who'd taken his girl to a nice secluded spot and who caught Mitchell playing the Peeping Tom.

That could hardly be the answer. The facts as Piper knew them pointed all the other way. The young couple who saw Mitchell go past with his dog heard only one person running away after Mitchell went into the river. One person meant that the Peeping Tom motive could be rejected.

Judging by the shock she had had the money motive could be eliminated, too. What was the real reason behind the quarrel Ogden overheard? The funny thing was that the first time she had shown any emotion was when she learned that her husband had been heavily insured. . . .

It was strange, too, that he must have put the policy where nobody could find it. Why should it be secretly hidden when he had already made a will in favour of his wife ?

He must have wanted her to inherit the insurance money even if he had had no more real feeling for her than she evidently had for him. . . . Or did the answer lie in the lost policy ?

Alice Mitchell said, " I've never had very much to do with business and, what with one thing and another, all this is getting me a bit confused. Why did Mr. Wheatley say I could leave everything in his hands ? It's not fair, it's not fair at all. What do I do if the insurance company try to get out of paying me ? "

" That's the last thing they'll want to do," Piper said. " You speak to your solicitor. He'll explain the position to you."

" He doesn't seem able to explain anything. He just treats me as if I was a child." She stood up and walked ahead of Piper into the hall.

When they reached the front door he thought she was going to offer to shake hands with him. Instead she left him to open the door himself and waited in silence until he was outside.

Then she said, " My husband didn't believe in borrowing money. We didn't spend much so there was never any need for him to get into debt. Supposing I was to tell the insurance company that the policy must've got burned by accident ? "

" If you were to sign a declaration to that effect," Piper said, " it would be helpful. What makes you think you might've destroyed it ? "

" Well . . ." She looked down at her hands. " I was getting rid of a lot of old papers a few months ago . . . old bills and things belonging to the shop and stuff like that and "—she took a quick breath and glanced up at him to catch his expression—" I remember something that might've been a policy. It was in a long envelope. The more I think of it the more I'm convinced that that's what happened."

It was a lie—a stupid, clumsy lie that no one knowing the circumstances could possibly believe. Piper said, " I advise you to discuss the matter with Mr. Wheatley before you make any kind of statement to the company. Here's my card. Please let me know if by any chance you're mistaken and the policy does turn up."

" Yes . . . yes, I will." She brought the card close to her eyes and her lips formed his name silently before she looked up at him again. " I'll let you know, Mr. Piper, without fail."

" Please do."

" But I don't think we'll find it. I'm sure it was destroyed. Anyway, Frank wouldn't borrow money . . . he wasn't the borrowing kind. We were married fifteen years, so I should know, shouldn't I ? "

" You should know," Piper said.

She gave him a brief nod, her eyes once more expressionless. Then she closed the door. As he walked down the path he heard her turn the key in the lock.

Outside number 11, Ogden was still clipping the privet hedge. He said, " Hello. . . . Find her in all right ? "

" Yes, thank you."

" Good. It would've been a pity to come all this way for nothing. Warm now, isn't it ? "

" Very warm," Piper said. " Weather seems to have settled down again . . . good-bye."

" Good-bye." The little man began using his shears once more. He was still busily clipping when Piper reached the corner and turned into Sion Road.

CHAPTER X

THERE WAS a meeting in Superintendent Mullett's office that afternoon. Both the Superintendent and Sergeant Pugh were interested in what Piper had to say about Mrs. Mitchell's reactions when she learned the size of her late husband's insurance policy, but the official view was that the interview provided no fresh evidence.

As Sergeant Pugh put it, " If she was genuinely surprised, sir, we can more or less eliminate her. In any case, there's been nothing from the very start to incriminate either her or her brother : nothing you could pin down, that is."

Superintendent Mullett was inclined to agree with him. ". . . I've had inquiries made in the neighbourhood of Douglas Crescent and also where she used to live, and we haven't come up with the slightest suggestion that there could be another man in it."

Piper said, " So she didn't have a motive, and her brother would've been crazy to let himself be seen at the house if he went out to Richmond that night with the intention of murdering Frank Mitchell."

" Assuming he had a reason for committing murder. If he had it's beyond me."

" Therefore it wasn't Alice Mitchell . . . or her brother . . . or that fellow Heald. And Mitchell didn't look prosperous enough to tempt someone to attack him for the sake of his money. Yet a man was more or less battered to death and then chucked in the river. So where do we go from here ? "

" We don't go anywhere," Mullett said. " These are early days yet. What I'd like to know right now is what's happened to that insurance policy for ten thousand pounds. If he didn't deposit it at his bank or with his lawyer, it should be at home."

Sergeant Pugh said, " I wonder if there's anything in

her story that she accidentally destroyed it along with some old papers."

"Rubbish. None of us really believes that. My opinion is that it'll turn up. What do you say, Mr. Piper?"

Piper said, "Let's assume he didn't borrow money on it. Then, if he entrusted it to someone other than his bank, his solicitor or his wife, he must've wanted to make quite sure it was safe. The question is—safe from whom? The only one who stood to benefit was his wife."

"If he didn't want it to get into her hands then"—the Superintendent felt his chin thoughtfully—"maybe he didn't intend her to have the money."

"Letting someone else hold the policy wouldn't affect his wife's right to inherit the money," Piper said.

Pugh cleared his throat. He said, "Perhaps he didn't want her to know he was heavily insured. This may sound silly, but perhaps he was afraid."

Superintendent Mullett threw down his pencil and stretched himself. He said, "This is where I came in. All roads lead to Rome . . . but the signposts point the other way."

"There may be another explanation for the missing policy," Piper said. "If and when it comes to light I have a feeling we'll understand better why Frank Mitchell was murdered. Not that I've anything to go on. It's just a feeling."

"I've got a feeling, too," Mullett said. He pushed himself to his feet and walked the length of the room and came back to his chair again. "Mine is that we're getting nowhere very fast."

"Too many loose ends . . . that's the trouble," Piper said. "There's one in particular that worries me. I'd like to know more about the man who's supposed to have assaulted Mrs. Coupland."

"That won't get you very far, sir," Pugh told him. "Take it from me she's in the same category as the dipsomaniac who walked into the station at Bermondsey and confessed that he'd done the job."

"You may be right, but I'd like to talk to her myself. Now I'll have to get back to the office. When I've got rid of my post I think I'll go and have a chat with the lady. . . ."

About half past four when he was almost ready to leave, he had a phone call from Mullett. The superintendent said, "Glad I caught you before you went out. I can save you making another trip to Richmond."

"How?"

"The statement made by Mrs. Edith Coupland was just a lot of nonsense. She's one of those psychopathic cases they've got a special name for. The kind that like to be the centre of attention and tell any tale so long as it gets them in the limelight for a while. What d'you call them?"

"Exhibitionists."

"That's right. Well, she's one. All that business about a man jumping out of nowhere and knocking her down and then dashing off isn't true . . . not a word of it. There's scarcely a murder case that doesn't have its quota of crack-pots. I've handled so many red herrings in my time I should be a member of the fishmongers' union."

"What's happened since I left your office that makes you so sure the story isn't true?"

"There's been another report from Crown Road police station. Seems that a constable on the beat near where she lives has just heard there was a minor accident outside one of the local shops the other day. A woman coming out of the grocer's was knocked down by some kid riding a bicycle on the pavement."

"Mrs. Coupland?"

"None other." The superintendent was sourly amused. "She wasn't hurt much. Banged her elbow and slightly grazed the palm of one hand. So there you are."

"Was this before or after the murder of Frank Mitchell?"

"The day after . . . on the Monday."

"No doubt that she got her injuries then and not the previous night on the river bank as she says?"

"Not to my mind. The grocer and his assistant helped her to her feet, saw she had hurt her hand, and heard her complain about her elbow. A couple of customers were in the shop at the time and they know about it, too. One of them lives not far from Mrs. Coupland. Walked home with her. The man on the beat got their names from the shopkeeper and the name of the child as well."

"It's fortunate that her story had very little real significance," Piper said. "And even more fortunate that the truth came to light before anything turned up that might've made us take her hocus-pocus seriously. What're you going to do now?"

"I could ask you the same question," Mullett said. "What can any of us do? Mitchell doesn't seem to have amounted to much while he lived, but he was worth ten thousand pounds soon's he died. And somebody caused his death. I'd say that means something, wouldn't you?"

"As an insurance assessor I can only look at it one way . . . until I'm proved wrong. It's as simple as that."

Superintendent Mullett said, "Sure, it's simple. But I've often found that the cases which look simple at first sight turn out to be the stickiest of all . . . and I think this is one of them. It might take us a long time to pin this job on somebody."

"My trouble is I haven't got time to spare," Piper said. "Mrs. Mitchell's solicitor will already have made application to the court. Soon's he gets the death certificate he'll apply for probate. Then he'll lodge a claim on the Cresset . . . and the company will have to pay up."

"Too bad. Don't think I'm unsympathetic, but I have troubles of my own which worry me more than ten thousand pounds worries the Cresset Insurance Company."

Piper said, "I have only one worry and that's to see no one gets away with money he or she isn't legally entitled to."

"Amen to that," Mullett said. "Just remember that my job is to see that nobody literally gets away with murder."

The following morning's post brought a letter unlike the rest of Piper's business correspondence arriving by the first delivery. It was in a small square envelope and the address had been crudely printed with a blunt pencil. According to the postmark it had been posted in Richmond at 5.45 p.m. the previous evening.

The letter itself consisted of a single square of paper cut to fit the size of the envelope. In the same style of block letters apparently with the same blunt pencil were the words :

YOU MIGHT BE INTERESTED TO KNOW MRS. MITCHELL WAS IN THE BEVERLEY NURSING HOME LAST YEAR FOR NEARLY SIX MONTHS.

That was all : just three printed lines without address or signature. As an anonymous letter it could hardly have been considered in the poison-pen class.

When he had re-read the letter and studied the postmark again Piper thought about a little man who had been clipping the hedge outside number 11 Douglas Crescent. There had been no sound of the shears when Mrs. Mitchell looked up from the visiting card and said, ". . . *I'll let you know, Mr. Piper, without fail.*"

. . . Ogden was only a few yards away and he could easily have heard her use his name. What else was it she had said ? ". . . *I don't think we'll find it. I'm sure it was destroyed. Anyway, Frank wouldn't borrow money . . . he wasn't the borrowing kind. . . .*"

There were about a hundred and fifty Pipers in the phone book, but Ogden would scarcely expect Mrs. Mitchell's visitor to be plumber or a marine engineer, a clothing manufacturer or a drysalters' warehouseman. Her parting remark would reduce the list considerably. Who was more likely to be calling on a newly-bereaved widow than an insurance assessor ?

It cost Ogden nothing even if he picked the wrong one. If his letter got to me all right he'd achieve his object . . . whatever that might be.

The Beverley Nursing Home was in Marksbury Avenue, Mortlake. It had a private branch exchange. Piper spent some time in thought before he made up his mind.

A woman's voice at the other end told him matron was out at the moment. Was there any message, please ?

Piper said, " This is the Ministry of Health. You had a patient for some months last year called Mitchell. The initial isn't very legible, but it looks like Mrs. F. Mitchell. We have a query about this woman. Could you get out your records and give me some information ? "

" Yes, sir, of course. If you'll hold the line . . . won't be a minute. . . ."

The clock on Piper's desk ticked away nearly three minutes before she came back to the phone. She said, " We had two Mitchells last year . . . but one was only in for a few weeks. It'll be the other one, I expect, that you're inquiring about. Her initial was F . . . and she was here from early January until nearly the end of June."

" That'll be the one," Piper said.

" What was it you wanted to know, sir ? "

" Well, the position is that a claim for sickness benefit has been referred to us for decision. We are querying the length of time she spent in the Beverley Nursing Home. It seems excessive for a maternity case."

. . . *Would an official of the Ministry of Health expect to obtain details by telephone ? At the worst she can only tell me I'll have to write to the matron. With a bit of luck. . . .*

The woman on the phone said, " But Mrs. Mitchell wasn't a maternity case."

" You must be looking at the wrong Mitchell," Piper said. " According to our information this woman gave birth to a daughter on the seventeenth of January last year."

" Then I'm afraid your information is wrong. She didn't have any baby here, I can assure you. We don't handle maternity cases."

" But this is absurd ! I have her papers in front of me and it says quite distinctly—"

" Whatever it says, it's wrong. I've got Mrs. Mitchell's admission card right here. Apart from anything else, this nursing home only takes patients suffering from nervous disorders. Mrs. Mitchell was a voluntary patient admitted for treatment on the advice of her doctor and a consultant psychiatrist."

" You mean she was a mental case ? "

Very stiffly, the phone said, " We never use that term here. If I remember correctly, Mrs. Mitchell was suffering from depression . . . quite a common thing in a woman of her age."

"This is a most peculiar business. . . . How old was she ?"

"According to the card she was forty-nine when admitted."

"And her address ?"

"Number 9 Douglas Crescent, Richmond."

"Same person, all right. Seems as if there's been a slip-up somewhere."

The phone said, "Not at this end. The patient underwent treatment and was discharged last June. Anything else I can tell you ?"

"No, thank you," Piper said. "Nothing else. You've been most helpful."

CHAPTER XI

A WEEK WENT BY—a week in which there were no developments of any kind. The police pursued their inquiries without material result : Piper asked a few discreet questions about a man called James Newton and then checked the financial standing of the business that had been owned by Frank Albert Mitchell.

Before the week was over he knew quite a lot about Mrs. Mitchell's husband and brother, but none of his information provided the slightest evidence that either brother or sister had had any part in what had happened on Sunday night, July the ninth.

Newton had been employed as a restaurant car attendant for close on five years. His superiors had always found him to be honest, conscientious and of sober habits. He performed his duties efficiently ; his general behaviour had never aroused any criticism ; he had an unbroken attendance record except for one week's absence due to a bout of 'flu for which he had presented a doctor's note.

In his domestic life he was equally respected. His rent was always paid up to date, local tradesmen looked on him as a steady, reliable customer whose requirements were small but who paid cash for what he bought. The portrait that Piper eventually pieced together was hardly that of a man who would have planned and carried out a cold-blooded and particularly brutal murder.

Frank Mitchell's business was also a model of respectability. It had never shown more than a modest profit, but all inquiries demonstrated that it had been financially sound at the time of its owner's death.

Piper told himself that Mitchell had had no reason to borrow money, no reason, therefore, to hand over his insurance policy as security for a loan. Furthermore, if he had ever wanted to raise money, he would obviously have approached his bank . . . but the bank had no knowledge of the policy.

Superintendent Mullett had been right about Alice Mitchell, too. Her reputation was impeccable.

Shopkeepers with whom she had dealt before moving to her present address respected her as a careful housewife who had never allowed herself to run into debt. Former neighbours who had known her for a number of years had never seen her in the company of any man other than her husband or her brother.

All Piper's inquiries led to only one conclusion. Three respectable people of unblemished character had become involved in murder through no fault of their own.

. . . *It seems ridiculous even to suspect either Mrs. Mitchell or her brother. Yet . . . one of these respectable people was done to death . . . By a stranger—without premeditation or prospects of gain? Or by someone who knew this man's life was insured for ten thousand pounds?*

By Monday morning, July the twenty-fourth, the newspapers had dropped the Richmond Murder story. Other news had taken its place.

There had been the usual holiday crop of seaside drownings . . . two schoolboys killed on a climbing expedition in Wales . . . a plane crash over the week-end with a toll of thirty-five lives. The public was no longer interested in what had happened to Frank Albert Mitchell.

At ten o'clock that morning Piper was reading the last of his correspondence when the phone rang. A man's voice asked, " Was it you who called at Mrs. Mitchell's house last week to talk about an insurance policy ? "

Piper said, " Yes. Who's that speaking ? "

" I'm her brother—Jim Newton. She asked me to give you a ring. I believe you wanted her to get in touch with you if "—he sounded slightly unsure of himself—" if she had any news about Frank's policy. Is that right ? "

" Yes, I did. Has she found it ? "

" Well, not exactly. But it seems it wasn't lost, after all. She thought you ought to know . . . because she gave you the idea it might've been burned with some old papers. Now it looks as if she must've been wrong."

" I'm very glad to hear it," Piper said. " Where is the policy ? "

Newton hesitated again. At last, he said, " Well, it's a bit difficult to explain. I don't quite understand what this is all about myself. I wasn't there when the woman came to see her so I'm not very clear . . ." His soft plaintive voice tailed off. He had his sister's habit of leaving conversation in mid-air.

Piper said, " I'm not at all clear about anything. Who is this woman you're talking about ? "

" I don't know her name, but she said she'd been sent by someone called Miss Scott. She wanted to know who the solicitor is who's handling Frank's estate because she hasn't got a solicitor of her own and she thought the one who's acting for my sister would know what to do—in the circumstances. That was yesterday afternoon. . . ."

" Why don't you start from the beginning ? " Piper said. " It's the quickest way in the long run."

" Yesterday afternoon is the beginning." He raised his voice as though he thought that might help. " I was out at Richmond last night and I heard about it . . . and I suggested we should tell you and hear what you had to say. That's why I'm phoning you. . . ." He dwindled off into silence again.

Piper said, " I'm afraid I don't follow you at all, Mr. Newton. Who is Miss Scott ? "

" She was once in service with Frank Mitchell's family . . . years ago when he was only a child. I think she was his nanny. My sister says he once mentioned something about her." As though it had some special significance, Newton added, " But not recently."

" Am I to understand that this Miss Scott's in possession of your brother-in-law's insurance policy ? "

" That's what she says—or at least it's what this other woman says. If it's true "—his voice faded and then recovered again—" it makes things kind of awkward."

" Why ? I'd have thought that finding the policy would've saved Mrs. Mitchell quite a lot of inconvenience."

" Well, no. The thing is my sister's afraid Mr. Wheatley'll be very annoyed with her."

" You'll have to explain what you mean by that," Piper told him. " I see no reason why Mr. Wheatley, or anyone else for that matter, should be annoyed because your sister's found a document that everybody's been looking for."

The phone went quiet. Then Newton said, " To be honest with you, my sister's done something she never should have done. If she'd asked me I'd have told her it was silly . . . but the first I heard of it was when I went to see her last night."

" What is it she's done ? "

" Well, you see, after you spoke to her she went to see Mr. Wheatley again and she swore an affidavit that she'd destroyed the policy by accident three or four months ago. Now, d'you understand ? "

" However foolish or wrong that may have been," Piper said, " it's entirely Mrs. Mitchell's affair. Mr. Wheatley may feel concerned on her behalf, but I'd hardly say he'd be annoyed. There's also the chance that he hasn't yet handed over the affidavit. If that is so, no harm will have been done."

" I've told her that, but she won't listen to me. She's always been scared of lawyers and people like that . . . so she asked me if I'd have a word with you. . . ."

A picture came into Piper's mind of a man who had met his death in the Thames on a peaceful summer's night —a man who had been cruelly beaten about the head so that he was probably blinded in one eye and losing consciousness. He had seen his dog struck down by a blow that had crushed its skull . . . and his only escape had been the river. . . .

Piper said, " Why should Mrs. Mitchell think I can do anything about it ? Her solicitor is the man to see. That was the advice I offered when I visited her at Richmond."

" Yes, she told me. But she says you sounded like a reasonable man . . . and she feels she could trust you."

" I appreciate the compliment but, if she can't trust Wheatley, it's time she got herself a new solicitor."

With something unpleasant behind his voice, Newton said, " One solicitor is no bigger rogue than the next. They're all out for what they can get. I haven't heard of one yet who wouldn't grab all he could lay his hands on."

" Your experience with the law seems to have been rather unfortunate," Piper said.

" It isn't the law that's to blame. It's the fellows who use the law to make money . . . and don't care two hoots about the client. . . . Will you hear what my sister has to say about this Miss Scott ? "

" Is there any more to tell ? "

" Yes, there's something I haven't mentioned. My sister thinks "—Newton's voice became softer—" that this might have something to do with Frank's death. Can I bring her to see you ? "

" Where are you speaking from now ? "

" The phone box near where I live at King's Cross. She's standing outside waiting for me."

" All right," Piper said. " I'd like to hear the rest of what happened yesterday. Bring your sister to my office . . . if that's what she wants."

" Thank you, sir. It's very good of you. We'll be there in about half an hour."

Mrs. Alice Mitchell was wearing flat-heeled black shoes, a black coat and black string gloves. Her dark green hat could hardly have been more unbecoming if she had specially chosen it to accentuate her pasty complexion. Her eyes were afraid, her manner that of a woman who was nervous and yet indignant.

Newton was a male version of the same type without being decidedly masculine. He carried his hat with a slightly affected air and he seemed to be just too correct.

When Piper pulled forward a couple of chairs, Mrs. Mitchell thanked him in a small colourless voice, sat down primly and tucked her feet out of sight. With both hands covering the handbag on her lap she gave him several little darting glances before she concentrated her attention on the window.

James Newton sat down and hitched up his trousers. Then he crossed his legs carefully so as not to spoil the crease, unfastened his jacket and tugged at the fronts to make himself comfortable. The suit he was wearing was not expensive but it was evidently his best one.

Piper said, " Before we start, Mrs. Mitchell, I do want you to bear in mind that I am at present employed by the Cresset Insurance Company. In other words, you mustn't expect me to treat what you tell me as confidential."

Without any emphasis, Alice Mitchell said, " The murder of my husband isn't confidential, either."

" Quite true. I just wanted you to appreciate my position. Now, what makes you think the information you received yesterday has any bearing on your husband's death ? "

" Because . . ." She took a long slow breath and let it out again. After a sidelong glance at her brother she began again.

" I got a shock yesterday, Mr. Piper, a very great shock. I never dreamed for a moment that Frank could do a thing like this to me. We were happily married for fifteen years. A woman's entitled to think she understands a man after all that time . . . isn't she ? "

It was a rhetorical question requiring no answer, but she seemed to expect one. Piper said, " Yes, I suppose so."

" Then why didn't he tell me what he was doing ? I was his wife . . . I was entitled to be consulted. If he was afraid I'd object, that was all the more reason why he shouldn't have kept it from me." She seemed to be struggling with a problem too great for her mind to grasp.

"What was it he kept from you?"

"He was keeping this other woman . . . that's what he was doing."

Newton stirred and made a pained face. He said, "You're exaggerating, Alice. You make it sound as if . . ." He gave Piper a little embarrassed smile and relapsed into silence.

"Usually it means only one thing when a wife discovers that her late husband has been keeping another woman," Piper said. "But the circumstances in this case appear to be somewhat different. If this Miss Scott was in service as a nanny to your husband's family when he was a child, she must've been considerably older than he was."

In a quiet, stubborn voice, Alice Mitchell said, "It doesn't matter how old she was. He had no right making her an allowance without getting my permission. And then to do a thing like this . . ." She shook her head and looked at Piper with no understanding in her eyes.

"Do a thing like what, Mrs. Mitchell?"

"He made a new will some time last year and left the money from his insurance policy to her."

Once again Piper thought of those last few moments on the river bank before Frank Mitchell disappeared in the darkness of the Thames. There had been the furious barking of his dog . . . then he had cried out: ". . . *No . . . no! Keep away! I'm warning you. . . .*"

Only a few seconds later the Scotch terrier had been battered to death and he was struggling in the water. From start to finish the whole thing had taken less than a minute.

. . . *Everything points to the fact that there must've been some preliminary conversation before his walking-stick was snatched from him. He must've been acquainted with the person who lay in wait for him. . . . It was known that he passed that spot at the same time every night. How many people knew it? If this new story is true. . . .*

Piper said, "I'd like to hear exactly what you were told by this woman who called on you yesterday."

Mrs. Mitchell touched her pale lips with the tip of her

tongue. She needed time to put her thoughts in order before she said, " I was just thinking I'd make myself a cup of tea . . . it'd be about three o'clock . . . when there was a knock at the door and this woman says she's been sent by Miss Scott who knew my late husband and she'd be obliged if I'd tell her who my solicitor is. I didn't know what she was talking about at first so I asked her to come in and explain and—"

" Just a moment," Piper said. " Did you get this woman's name ? "

" Yes. She said she was a Miss Reid. I got the idea she did some kind of work for Miss Scott by the way she spoke."

" Why hadn't Miss Scott called on you herself ? "

" She wasn't able to for some reason."

" I see. Go on, please."

" Well "—Mrs. Mitchell wet her lips again—" she had asked Miss Reid to say she hoped I wouldn't be upset because Frank had left her this money. It had been his wish . . . and she hoped I'd see it that way."

" When had she last seen your husband ? "

" I didn't ask. It wasn't important after I'd just heard he'd given her the policy to keep for him and he'd also made out a new will and left it with her, too. I can't believe it even now. . . ."

She looked down at her gloved hands and then stared up at Piper with bewilderment in her eyes. " It wasn't in Frank to do a thing like that. I was a good wife to him for fifteen years . . . it's not bad enough that he was keeping this woman behind my back, but he has to go and rob me of the bit of comfort I might've had when I was left all alone with no one to support me."

A touch of colour came into her sallow cheeks. She turned and looked at her brother and asked, " Why should some old woman get ten thousand pounds when I'm left with only a little shop that I don't know anything about ? I might not even be able to sell it."

Newton glanced at Piper and said, " It doesn't seem right, does it ? "

" I'm in no position to question your brother-in-law's

motives," Piper told him. "Nor do I pretend to understand them. However, provided he fully realised what he was doing and this later will was properly executed . . . I presume it is of more recent date than the one in Mr. Wheatley's possession?"

Very dully, Mrs. Mitchell said, "She told me—this Miss Reid told me—that he made it out about twelve months ago. The will that Mr. Wheatley's got has been in his safe for years . . . at least nine or ten years."

"Have you spoken to Mr. Wheatley yet about the visitor you had yesterday?"

"No. I'm always scared of lawyers. And after"—she swallowed and her eyes became childishly guilty—"after signing a paper to say I'd burned the policy I daren't go back and tell him it wasn't true . . . because Frank gave it to some other woman. . . ."

Resentment drew down the corners of her mouth. "He cheated me. I'll never know why, but that's just what he did: he cheated me."

Piper said, "Did this woman Reid explain why Miss Scott didn't come forward as soon as she learned of your husband's death?"

"Miss Reid says they didn't get to know about it until yesterday."

"But it was in all the papers over a week ago. I wonder how it is that they've only just heard the news?"

Newton gave Piper a sly little look and murmured, "I wondered about that, too." He seemed pleased that they both shared the same thought.

Piper said, "My only interest in your husband's affairs, Mrs. Mitchell, concerns the life policy he took out with the Cresset Insurance Company. If the policy really is in the possession of this woman, Miss Scott, and she can present it when called upon to do so, there will be nothing to stop the company from paying the sum assured to your husband's estate. What happens to the money after that is entirely between you and Miss Scott. It's a matter for the lawyers to thrash out. You'll have to see what Mr. Wheatley thinks about it."

Mrs. Mitchell turned her head slightly to look at her

brother. Then her slow eyes returned to Piper's face. She said, " If Frank could do this to me he deserved what happened to him. All these years——"

" That's a terrible thing to say," Newton broke in. He was watching Piper anxiously.

Without looking at him, Alice Mitchell said, " Maybe it is . . . but it was a terrible thing he did to me. Maybe a punishment came on him for being so wicked. Maybe he'd have had a more peaceful end if he hadn't put temptation in somebody's way. . . ."

Her eyes drifted to the window and she sat very still as though listening to something that only she could hear. When she looked at Piper again, she said, " I'm not a clever woman. If I had been, perhaps none of this would ever have happened. But one thing I do know. . . ." She swallowed the rest and smiled to herself.

Piper said, " Yes ? "

" Frank wasn't very clever, either, was he ? "

With a trace of impatience in his voice, Newton said, " Mr. Piper isn't interested in how you felt about Frank . . . or how he felt about you for that matter. I only brought you here so he could tell us what he thought the insurance company would do about that affidavit you signed. Because you shouldn't have done it. You know that, don't you ? "

He spoke as if he were remonstrating with a child. Then both of them stared at Piper.

" As far as I can say at the moment," Piper said, " no harm appears to have been done. But the man you really must talk to is your solicitor, Mr. Wheatley. I'm not a lawyer, Mrs. Mitchell. Even if I were, I couldn't act for you in this or any other matter connected with your late husband's estate. I'm employed by the Cresset Insurance Company. You must understand that."

Alice Mitchell said, " I understand." The hint of venom that had been in her face when she spoke of her husband had gone. " I'll go and see Mr. Wheatley."

" Good. Tell him all about Miss Scott and the possibility that a later will exists. He'll want to talk to you in any case when he hears from Miss Scott. You gave Miss Reid his name, I suppose ? "

" Yes . . . yes, I did. I couldn't see any reason why I shouldn't."

" No reason at all."

Mrs. Mitchell and her brother stood up at the same time as if there was an affinity of mind between them. They had reached the door when Piper said, " Would you care to leave me Miss Scott's address ? "

" Oh, yes. I'd meant to give it to you . . . but I forgot." She opened her handbag and brought out a piece of paper that looked like a page torn from a pocket diary.

With no change of tone, she asked, " Will you make a copy of it so I can give this to Mr. Wheatley ? I haven't a very good head for names and addresses and phone numbers . . . and things like that. Why do you want it, anyway ? "

" It's for the company's files," Piper said. " They'll want to make a note of it."

He knew they would accept the answer like they had accepted all his other answers, some of which had been largely nonsense. Intelligent people would not have needed his ponderous advice. Alice Mitchell and her brother were not intelligent people.

. . . *But she seems the more stupid of the two. Her mind seems to wander . . . and somewhere in her there's a touch of viciousness. . . .*

As he returned the slip of paper, Alice Mitchell said, " How do I know this Miss Scott is the same one who was Frank's nanny ? "

" She'll have to establish her identity before they grant probate of the will," Piper said.

" Oh, maybe she'll be able to do that all right, but that doesn't mean to say she was ever in service with his mother. She might be some fancy woman who talked him into making a new will." With a thin bitter mouth, Mrs. Mitchell added, " They say there's no fool like an old fool. I'm beginning to understand lots of things I should've seen long ago. It must be true that a wife's the last one to find out."

In that moment before she left his office, Piper realised the kind of life Frank Albert Mitchell had lived before death struck him down swiftly and savagely while he was enjoying his evening walk along the river bank. If he had sought and found consolation elsewhere it was not to be wondered at. The little man, Ogden, might not have been exaggerating when he had talked about the sound of quarelling from the house next door.

As if sensing some change in Piper's attitude, James Newton said, " Frank's dead now, Alice. Don't go on about him this way. Mr. Piper doesn't want to hear things like that. He's not interested."

" Nobody's interested," Mrs. Mitchell said. " That's the trouble. I've had to keep it bottled up inside me all these years. You should know that."

They went out. As the door closed, she was saying in the same toneless voice, ". . . All he ever did was neglect me. I might as well not have been there half the time. When he died I thought I'd have no more aggravation. Now there's this. . . ."

Newton pushed the door shut hurriedly. Their footsteps receded along the corridor and down the stairs. In the distance her voice went on complaining about the woman to whom her husband had left a legacy of ten thousand pounds.

CHAPTER XII

KINGSMOUNT AVENUE, Forest Hill, was a long curving road with sycamore trees and neat grass verges on either side. Most of the houses were substantial detached villas with here and there a picturesque bungalow.

Miss Scott lived in a bungalow. Her home was not quite so large as the others, but the garden was well tended, the paintwork shining, the net curtains crisp and white. Clumps of nasturtium grew in profusion on either side of the doorway, their orange flowers spilling over on to the path.

The woman who opened the door was dark-haired, neat and unobtrusive. She had small features and small well-shaped hands. If she had worn suitable make-up and a more becoming hairstyle she would have been quite attractive. Piper guessed she was about thirty, perhaps a little older.

He said, " Good afternoon. I represent the Cresset Insurance Company. Is Miss Scott at home ? "

She smiled politely and without much warmth. In a pleasant voice, she said, " Will you come in, please ? " She sounded younger than she looked.

He went past her into the tiny hall and turned to watch her close the door. If this was Miss Reid she was hardly the type of person he had expected to meet. The impression he had gained from Mrs. Mitchell was of someone different. How different, he would have been unable to explain.

When she came away from the door, she asked, " What is your name, please ? "

" Piper, John Piper."

" Did you say the Cresset Insurance Company ? "

" That's right."

" If you'll wait here a moment, I'll tell Miss Scott. . . ." With another polite little smile she went into a room on the left of the hall and closed the door very quietly behind her.

He stood passing his hat from one hand to the other while he looked around at the old-fashioned carved mirror on the wall near the front door, the copper warming-pan hanging on another wall, the little table with a bunch of flowers in a glass vase, the carpet showing signs of wear in places.

. . . *Mitchell doesn't seem to have made Miss Scott a substantial allowance. He was forty-something so she must be over sixty. . . . Between what he gave her and her old age pension she's probably able to get by. Maybe she managed to save a little money in the days when she acted as a nanny. . . .*

. . . *Something ridiculous about the thought that she could've had anything to do with his death, insurance or no insurance. Just the kind of thing someone like Alice Mitchell would think of. . . .*

In the room on his left he could hear voices. One was the voice of the neat, dark-haired woman.

. . . *She could look quite pretty if she got herself a new dress and had a hair-do and made up her face a little. . . .*

Wonder why she works for Miss Scott? There can't be any money in it. Should be easy enough these days to get herself a better-paid job. Of course, she might be some relation of the old woman's. . . .

Then the murmuring voices stopped and the door opened. She said, " Will you come in, please ? "

It was a bright room, perhaps in need of re-decorating, but pleasant and homely. The furniture, like the pieces in the hall, belonged to a previous generation.

There was a small carved escritoire, a three-piece suite covered in some faded floral design, a walnut corner stand on which stood a vase of flowers and a silvered model of a horse, a low cabinet beside the hearth that probably contained a coal scuttle. Another vase of flowers gave a touch of colour to a corner on the other side of the fireplace.

On the tiled ledge above the hearth stood a set of figures representing a shepherd and a shepherdess, a reading lamp with a Japanese shade, a hand-cut wooden figure of an Assyrian lion. Everything was clean and shining and evidently much-loved.

In a chair just out of reach of the sunshine streaming through the window sat a thin, shrunken woman with almost white hair and eyes sunk deep in her head. Her face and hands were emaciated, her skin yellow and shrivelled. Whatever she might once have been she was now little more than a bright-eyed skeleton in a dress that hung on her loosely.

The dark-haired woman said, " This is the gentleman from the Cresset Insurance Company, Miss Scott. Do you want me to stay . . . or shall I go and make some tea ? "

Miss Scott gave Piper her hand and said, " How d'you do. . . . You will have a cup of tea, won't you ? I don't often get visitors . . . and tea's very refreshing on a hot day like this."

Piper said, " It's very kind of you. So long as you're not making it specially for me. . . ."

" Oh, no, no, not at all. We usually have a cup about this time . . . don't we, Joan ? . . . Oh, by the way, Mr. Piper, this is Miss Reid, my companion . . . and my very good friend."

Miss Reid smiled . . . and Piper said, " How d'you do. . . ." Then she murmured something about going to put the kettle on. With a little nod she went out.

When the door closed, Miss Scott said, " Sit down, Mr. Piper, sit down. . . . Now, tell me what brings you here."

" I thought I'd like to talk to you about Frank Mitchell," Piper said.

Her sunken eyes closed for a moment and her lips moved silently as though she were saying something to herself. Then she looked at him and made a little husky sound in her throat. She said, " Yes, of course. Poor Frank. . . . He was always a very reserved little boy. Never confided at all in people . . . even his own family. But he came to me when he was in trouble. I seemed to understand him better than his own mother. Does that seem strange to you ? "

" No, I've often heard that a child can become very attached to his nanny," Piper said.

" Yes, Frank was very attached to me. I had other boys after I left the Mitchell family, but Frank remained my favourite." She took a handkerchief from her sleeve and dabbed her mouth and then sighed. " I didn't see much of him for quite a number of years after he left boarding school because he went abroad . . . did you know that ? "

" No, I don't know much about him at all," Piper said.

When she had dabbed her mouth again, Miss Scott sat twisting the handkerchief between her bony fingers. Her skin had felt dry and cold when she shook hands with him. The touch of it had been unpleasant.

At last, she said, " He came to see me quite a lot after he came back." She was still smiling faintly, but Piper thought there were signs of pain in her haggard face. " Did you know his mother left me this house ? "

" No, I wasn't aware of that, either."

" You'd have liked her : she was a nice woman . . . a very nice woman. If it hadn't been for all the kindness she and Frank showed me "—Miss Scott moved painfully and the look of suffering deepened in her eyes—" I don't know what would've happened to me after I took ill."

"I'm sorry I've had to trouble you," Piper said. "I know this must be a very trying time and—"

"Oh, don't apologise, please. You have your job to do, no doubt . . . and I like visitors, anyway. I get so very few, you know." She sighed again. "When I couldn't get around any more I asked Frank once or twice if he'd fetch his wife to see me. She didn't come, of course. I hadn't really expected she would. . . . Have you met—Mrs. Mitchell?"

"Yes, I called on her the other day," Piper said. "It was she who gave me your name and address. She told me about the conversation she'd had with Miss Reid."

"Is she very upset about thc new will?"

"In the circumstances I doubt if any wife wouldn't be upset. Ten thousand pounds is a lot of money for a man to leave to some other woman. She also feels her husband had no right to keep it secret that he was making you an allowance."

"Didn't she know? Oh, dear . . ." Miss Scott drew in her thin bloodless mouth and looked hurt. "That was certainly wrong of him, very wrong, indeed. But I suppose he knew she wouldn't agree to it . . . and he liked me, Mr. Piper. He was as good to me as any son could've been. Without those few pounds a week I don't know what I'd have done. I certainly wouldn't have been able to pay Miss Reid, and I had to have someone to look after me."

"He wasn't a rich man," Piper said. "And it wasn't only the allowance. His insurance premiums must've represented a considerable drain on his income."

"So she feels she's been robbed," Miss Scott said. "I don't really blame her. After all, she wasn't to know when she married him that she wouldn't make him the right kind of wife."

Somewhere not far away a door opened. Piper heard the rattle of dishes. He said, "Why did Frank Mitchell marry her?"

Miss Scott shook her head slowly from side to side. With sadness sharpening the bones of her face, she said, "Why does any man marry any woman? They say God sorts them out in pairs. . . . This was a very bad match, Mr. Piper, a very bad match. He rarely talked about his wife, but I've known for a long time that he was unhappy. Poor boy . . . poor, dear boy. . . ."

"Did he dislike his wife so much that he had to punish her by leaving all this money to you ?"

"Oh, no, you're quite wrong. You mustn't think that." Miss Scott was profoundly shocked. "His wife is provided for. She's quite young and she has a well-established business. There's no reason why she shouldn't be comfortably off. If she had more than she needed it's quite likely. . . ."

The door opened and Miss Reid came in carrying a tray with cups and saucers and a pewter tea service. She said, "Excuse me. . . ." Her smile came and went swiftly when Piper got up and brought over a small table to stand between Miss Scott's chair and his own.

When she had put down the tray, she asked, "Shall I pour out for you . . . or will you manage yourself ?"

Miss Scott said, "Won't you stay and have a cup of tea with us ? We're not discussing anything private, are we, Mr. Piper ?"

Piper said, "No, nothing private at all. I'd be very pleased if Miss Reid would join us."

He thought he could hear small sounds of movement in another room, two or three footsteps on an uncarpeted floor. The fact that there was a third member of the household was not nearly so interesting as the impression he had that the footsteps were those of a man.

Miss Reid said, "No, thank you. If you don't mind, I won't. I've got—something to do. So, if you'll excuse me . . ." Without looking at him she went out again.

She left the door slightly ajar this time. A moment or two later, her footsteps joined those of the man in the other room.

With some difficulty Miss Scott poured tea. Her hands were no more than skin and bone and they had scarcely enough strength to lift the teapot.

Piper sat watching her with pity. In years she was not an old woman, but suffering had aged her. Illness had bleached the life out of her until now she was merely a shell in which pain had made its home.

He waited until she had taken two or three bird-like sips from her cup before he said, " You were saying that Mrs. Mitchell would've had more than her needs demanded if her husband had left her this money. . . ."

" Was I ? " She held her shaking cup between both hands and looked up at him doubtfully. " Well, I shouldn't say things like that. It's none of my business. I don't want to bore you with my silly ideas."

" You're not boring me in the least," Piper said.

She took another sip and closed her eyes while she swallowed it. Then she gave him a travesty of a smile. Without any feeling, she said, " I'm a sick woman, Mr. Piper, a very sick woman."

Piper said, " I'm sorry. Perhaps I've kept you talking too long. Rather than have you overtire yourself I suggest——"

" No, no, don't go away. I'm all right . . . quite all right. Having somebody to talk to is a real treat for me. Ordinarily, the only person I see is the nurse who comes each morning." As though it meant nothing, she added, " I get morphia every day."

Piper told himself that the answer to the murder of Frank Mitchell must lie elsewhere. The key to the riddle was not in this house where a woman had to be given daily injections of morphine to deaden her pain.

He said, " How long have you been suffering like this, Miss Scott ? "

" Oh, a long time now . . . such a long time." She put down her cup and wiped her mouth with the handkerchief. In her eyes lay the resignation that comes when all hope is gone.

Very simply, she said, " It's only morphia that makes my life bearable. I've got cancer of the stomach."

" Is there nothing they can do—apart from drugs ? "

" Nothing now—merely to give me these injections every day. And that's only to ease the pain so that I can die in reasonable comfort. When I eventually went to a doctor it was too late. . . ."

She shrugged and tried to smile, but the effort was pathetic. " Oh, they did their best. I had what they called a partial gastrectomy . . . but it didn't do any good. The trouble had gone too far."

To offer sympathy would have been presumptuous. Piper said, " Did they tell you nothing more could be done ? "

" Oh, yes, there's no question about it, no question at all." She folded her fleshless hands around the handkerchief and looked at him steadily. In a clear distinct voice, she said, " I shall be dead in less than a year . . . probably much less. Certainly a year is the very most that I've got left."

Through the partly open door Piper could hear two people talking. One was the dark-haired woman, the other was a man. It seemed that the duties which had prevented Miss Reid from sharing a cup of tea were not of a very pressing nature.

He said, " To be able to discuss it like this, Miss Scott, you must be a very brave woman. Did Frank Mitchell know what you've just told me ? "

Her hesitation was slight but noticeable. " Yes, he learned after the operation that there was no hope of a cure. Up to then I'd been working. I should've gone to see a doctor earlier, I suppose, but I've never had much time for people who fuss over their health. So I didn't seek advice until people began telling me I was losing weight. . . ."

There her voice became a thin thread of sound. She lay back in the chair and closed her eyes and the hollows in her sunken cheeks became even more pronounced.

Piper said, " I'd better leave you now. You mustn't overtire yourself. I'll call Miss Reid on my way out."

Very faintly, she said, " No . . . no, don't go. I'll be all right in a moment. It'll pass. . . ."

He waited . . . and listened to the voices in the other room . . . and wondered what would happen to Miss Scott's money when she died.

Then her eyes opened and she took a quivering breath and tried to smile. She said, " It's gone—for the time being. Please have another cup of tea . . . if you don't mind helping yourself."

"I shouldn't be here drinking tea with you," Piper said. "It must be distressing for you to talk about Frank Mitchell in view of the way you felt about him. You need rest. Wouldn't it be better if I were to come back in a day or two? It wouldn't be any trouble, I assure you."

In a stronger voice, she said, "No, I'm all right now. And one of these days"—there was no melancholy in the difficult little smile she gave him—"I'll get plenty of rest. Until then I want to live and talk to people and forget for a little while that I've only got a little while. Unless you have another appointment and must get away?"

"No, I'm not in any hurry," Piper said.

"Good." She eased herself more upright in her chair and studied him almost critically. "You know, Mr. Piper, you make a very good audience. You came here to talk about Frank and I've done nearly all the talking. No wonder my husband says we don't need a wireless set in this house."

Something in his face seemed to amuse her. When she had tucked the handkerchief into her sleeve, she went on, "You look surprised. What have I said? . . . Oh, of course, you didn't know I was married. Nannies are never married, are they?"

"I was told your name was Miss Scott," Piper said. "And that's how Miss Reid referred to you, also. It must've been your husband's voice I heard in another room a few moments ago. I wondered who the man was."

"Yes, Alan's got the afternoon off . . . so he thought he'd make himself useful by painting the kitchen." With an air of strange simplicity, she added, "My name's really Mrs. Clark, you know, but I was always called Nanny or Miss Scott and I've gone on thinking of myself that way. A lifetime's habit is very difficult to break, especially"—a shadow seemed to come into her eyes—"when you try to take up married life again—too late."

Piper said, "Forgive me, but I've been wondering why you needed an allowance from Frank Mitchell if you had a husband able to support you."

"My husband was away for a number of years. His job kept him travelling about and he had a lot of expense . . . so he couldn't very well provide me with any money. Besides, I was working for myself until the beginning of this year. I didn't need anybody's help."

She was lying. Piper knew that beyond question. But there was something peculiar in her manner behind the lie. She was not at all worried although she must have known that the story about her husband's job away from home was too flimsy to be believed.

. . . *It's obvious he left her. Or maybe they agreed to separate. Now he's come back . . . because by some means he found out that she'd come into a substantial legacy when Frank Mitchell died. Is the problem of Mitchell's death not really a problem at all ?*

The thought loomed frighteningly in Piper's mind as he looked at the woman who had only a few months to live. At last, he said, "I'd like you to tell me about the insurance policy and the will, Miss Scott. Do you know why they were left with you instead of being put in the safekeeping of his lawyer as is the customary thing to do ?"

"He didn't trust his lawyer," Miss Scott said. Her sunken eyes told Piper that this was certainly the truth. "Frank didn't want to run the risk that his wife would get to hear about the new will."

"Why didn't he want his wife to know ?"

"Because she'd have made his life a misery."

"Is that what he told you ?"

"He never discussed the matter with me . . . but I'm now able to draw my own conclusions. At the time I didn't know what was in the envelope he asked me to keep for him. It was sealed."

"When did you find out what it contained ?"

"Only a few days ago. After I heard"—she looked down at the tea tray and her lips trembled—"what had happened."

"I'm rather puzzled about that," Piper said. "There was quite a lot in the papers about the man who was murdered at Richmond, and a few days later they gave the story fresh prominence when his identity became known. Yet you didn't get to hear of it until a day or two ago. How is that ?"

Miss Scott looked at him and took a long time to answer. Her sunken eyes seemed to be probing deep into his mind. Then she said, "You're a detective . . . aren't you ?"

To give her an evasive answer seemed cheap. Piper said, "Not perhaps in the way you mean. My ordinary job is to act as an assessor when claims are made. In this case, the Cresset Insurance Company have asked me to make inquiries into the circumstances of Frank Mitchell's death. But I'm not any kind of policeman, Miss Scott."

She chewed her lips and went on staring at him. Then she said, "What do they think you can do that the police can't ?"

"So far as Mitchell's killer is concerned, probably nothing. But the company feels a little happier when it has someone like me keeping a watching brief on their behalf as it were."

"You mean they think there might be some reason why they shouldn't pay the money ?"

"Personally, I hope there isn't. But you do appreciate that this isn't just an ordinary case of payment by an insurance company on the death of the insured party. When a man who's been insured for ten thousand pounds is murdered, any insurance company is bound to ask questions that they wouldn't normally dream of asking."

"And that's why you're here ?"

"That's why I'm here," Piper said.

Miss Scott nodded. Her small deep-sunk eyes seemed to be looking in on her own mind as she asked, "What will you tell your company now that you've spoken to me ?"

"I haven't decided yet."

"What are you still doubtful about ?"

"Mitchell knew what you've just told me about the state of your health. He knew, therefore, it was most unlikely that he would predecease you. Although he had several months in which to alter the will he'd made in your favour he didn't do so. Why ?"

"Perhaps he didn't think of it. I know I forgot all about the envelope he'd left here until my husband came across it in one of the drawers over there." She pointed to the little escritoire. "He wouldn't have mentioned it, either, if I hadn't said I couldn't understand why Frank hadn't been to see me for the past couple of weeks."

She rubbed her cold dry hands together. They made a sound like the rustle of dead leaves. "That was when he told me—what had happened."

"I suppose your husband had tried to avoid breaking the news."

"Yes. When he realised he couldn't go on keeping it from me there was nothing else to do but tell me that Frank—was dead. After I'd got over the first shock, he suggested I should open the envelope."

"Was that the first time it had been opened?"

She took too long to answer. Then she said, "Yes, of course."

"Were you very surprised to discover that Frank had left you such a large sum of money?"

"When you sit like I do counting the days, nothing can surprise you." She fumbled for the handkerchief in her sleeve and dabbed her mouth again. "I didn't try to understand it because the money means nothing to me. I'd give it all for one day's freedom from pain."

Now she meant what she was saying. The sincerity in her voice left no room for any doubt.

Piper said, "You were in his confidence, Miss Scott. Did he ever mention that he had an enemy, that he was afraid someone might try to do him harm?"

"No, never. He wasn't the kind of man to make enemies. He got on well with almost—everybody."

"Almost but not quite everybody. Someone caused his death, Miss Scott. Someone must've been waiting on the river bank that night with the express purpose of committing murder. That person killed a man who'd been good to you in many ways. In fact, everyone I've spoken to says that Frank Mitchell was a quiet-living, good-natured fellow. Why should anyone want to beat him to death?"

Miss Scott said, "I don't know. I've lain awake thinking about it over and over again, but I still don't know." Her lips trembled and there was grief in her haggard face. " He always meant as much to me as if he'd been my own child. I saw him become more and more unhappy as time went by . . . they gave him no peace . . . he had no life of his own. . . ."

Tears filled her eyes. She used her handkerchief roughly as though angry with herself.

" You're referring to his wife and her brother, I suppose," Piper said.

She sat wiping her eyes until she had regained composure. Then she said, " Alice Mitchell's brother meant more to her than her husband. I was never able to understand it, but Frank took second place in everything. She's absolutely devoted to that brother of hers. Never seemed to realise how lucky she was to get a man like Frank. If only my husband had been the steady type who knew how to stay out of trouble. . . ."

As she put her handkerchief away Miss Scott looked at Piper guiltily. In an awkward voice, she added, " I shouldn't talk about Alan like that . . . it's wrong of me. Everybody makes mistakes. He's been very good to me since he "—she stumbled momentarily—" since he came home. If it weren't for him I couldn't face the next few months."

Once again Piper told himself she was lying. He would have classed her as a normally truthful person who found it uncomfortable to lie. When a woman had such a short time to live what did she expect to achieve by concealing the truth ?

. . . *By throwing suspicion on Mrs. Mitchell and her brother she hopes she's deflecting it from someone else. And the someone else can be only one person. Now there's a question I've got to ask. Trouble is how on earth am I to put it* . . . ?

He said, " Have you still got the insurance policy and the will ? "

" No, no, I haven't. Miss Reid took them to Mr. Wheatley's office this morning." After a short pause, Miss Scott murmured, " My husband thought that was the best thing to do in the circumstances. It was . . . wasn't it ? "

" If you haven't a solicitor of your own there's no reason why you shouldn't use Mr. Wheatley. While we're on the subject of wills. . . ."

" Yes ? "

" Have you considered making one since you heard about the legacy that Frank Mitchell left you ? "

Miss Scott said, " Why, I made my will long ago. Soon's I came out of hospital after my operation I bought one of those printed forms and filled it in. It's been in one of those drawers ever since that time—until this morning, that is."

" Did you send it to Mr. Wheatley along with the other papers ? "

" Yes. I got a sudden fear it might not be really legal. Didn't matter six months ago when I had only this house and a few bits and pieces to leave. But now "—she chewed her lips as though she had something in her mouth —" now that I've got all this money, I don't want Joan to have any trouble after I'm gone. I've left everything to her, you know, because of the way she's looked after me."

Piper said, " I see." The relationship between Miss Scott and her husband was becoming clearer every moment.

" A will that's not drawn up properly can cause trouble afterwards, can't it ? " She seemed reluctant to leave the point as though her other thoughts had been side-tracked.

" It certainly can," Piper said. " You were wise to have it checked by a solicitor."

He had the answer to his question without having to ask it. As he stood up, he said, " Now, I really must go. Thank you for being so tolerant with me, Miss Scott."

" Not at all. I wish I could've done more." With no real curiosity in her voice, she asked, " Will you be coming to see me again ? "

" Possibly. If and when I do, I hope you'll be feeling much better."

Miss Scott said, " You're very kind. I've enjoyed our talk so much. . . ."

Her eyes followed him to the door. She smiled at him when he looked back at her. " Goodbye, Mr. Piper. . . . Oh, will you see yourself out or shall I ring for Miss Reid ? "

" Oh, no, don't go to any trouble. She's probably busy. I'll find my own way. . . ."

Miss Scott was still smiling at him faintly as he went out into the hall. His last glimpse of her before he closed the door told Piper that in one thing at least she could hardly be deceiving him. The grey cast of death already lay on her face.

For a moment he stood in the hall staring at his reflection in the mirror. The quiet voices in a room opposite were still talking.

He heard the man's voice say ". . . long to wait. This way of living is getting me down."

Very softly, Miss Reid said, " Hush . . . don't speak so loudly or they'll hear you. . . ."

Then there were sounds of a brief struggle and she complained, " No, Alan . . . please . . . you mustn't. If he looks in and sees us. . . . Wait until he's gone. . . . Oh, darling, darling. . . ."

After that there were only fugitive sounds which told Piper all he needed to know. On silent feet he walked to the partly-open door and glanced in quickly.

Miss Reid was in the arms of a man who was kissing her—a good-looking man with strong features and a well-shaped head and dark hair streaked with grey at the temples. Her hands were clasped behind his neck, her body strained against his in response.

It lasted only another moment and then she broke away from him. As she pushed herself free, Piper ducked back out of sight.

He could hear their voices again as he tiptoed to the front door. Without looking back he went out on to the porch and pulled the door shut behind him.

The click of the latch was loud, but it made no difference if they heard the door close. It would merely tell them he had gone. Only Miss Scott might wonder why it had taken him so long to leave.

Detective-Superintendent Mullett was not available at five-thirty. He was expected back soon. Piper phoned again shortly before six. The superintendent had gone home without apparently learning that someone had been inquiring for him.

So far as Piper was concerned there was no hurry to take any action. Neither Alan Clark nor Miss Reid would run away. They had to stay where they were until Miss Scott inherited the legacy left to her by Frank Mitchell. After that they would only need to wait for her to die.

Dr. O'Toole was an old friend. He asked no unnecessary questions and he provided confirmation if confirmation had been needed.

". . . From your description, Piper, I'd say she's got carcinoma of the stomach, all right. Sounds like the typical cachectic appearance of the cancer sufferer. Pronounced emaciation . . . sunken eyes . . . a loose, dry skin. In every instance the complexion's extremely pale. Sometimes it's tinged with yellow, as in this woman's case."

" How long would you say she'll live ? "

" Well, if they did a gastrectomy some months ago and that didn't do the trick, the prognosis is bad. I'd say she's got maybe another six months. Difficult to give you an opinion like this without seeing the patient for myself. Did you say they're giving her morphine daily ? "

" So she told me."

" M-m-m. . . . Did you notice if the pupils of her eyes were contracted ? "

" Yes, they were very small."

" Then it all adds up to the fact that the poor lass wasn't kidding you, old man. Shouldn't have been told that she'd only a year to live, of course. Then again she might've found out herself . . . they often do."

" I take it nobody would be surprised if she died any time from now on ? "

" A case of that kind might live six months, six weeks or six days. All a doctor can do is estimate a maximum time-limit. In January the disease had already progressed to a stage where operative treatment proved useless. I'd say twelve months from that time would be a fair expectation."

" So there'd be no questions asked, no suggestion of holding a post mortem if the patient were to die in her sleep one night in the near future ? "

" None whatsoever. What point are you trying to make ? "

" She'll shortly inherit a legacy of ten thousand pounds," Piper said. " I have a feeling that somebody will be too impatient to wait for Nature to take its course. And a pillow held over a sick woman's face could speed matters up considerably without a certain party running the slightest risk."

Dr. O'Toole said, " You know the nicest people, old man. Good night. . . ."

CHAPTER XIII

TUESDAY MORNING, July twenty-fifth, was warm and cloudy with only an occasional glimpse of the sun. The weather report forecast the possibility of thundery showers later in the day.

A few minutes after nine o'clock Piper phoned Superintendent Mullett's office again. He was told the superintendent might not yet have arrived . . . would he hold the line . . . ?

Then Mullett said, " Believe you were trying to get in touch with me last night. Just seen a note on my desk that says you rang a couple of times around six o'clock. What can I do for you ? "

" I had a visit yesterday morning from two people you know," Piper said. " They gave me some information that sent me off to see a lady who's married but who prefers to be known as Miss Muriel Scott. Ever heard of her ? "

" No. What is she ? "

" Many years ago she was Nanny to a small boy called Frank Albert Mitchell. Then she married a man who doesn't seem to have been much good as a husband. Now, she's a sick old woman with not much longer to live."

" What has her unfortunate marriage and breakdown in health to do with the life and death of Frank Mitchell ? "

" Quite a lot. If Miss Scott's erring husband hadn't

come back to her in recent months, it's possible that Mitchell might still be alive."

"Indeed!" Mullett said. "Why don't you come round here and tell me all about it? I've a piece of news that you may find interesting, too."

Whitehall was hot and dusty, the air stifling in the confines of Cannon Row. Beyond the listless trees on the Embankment the Thames surged darkly under Westminster Bridge.

Mullett had his window wide open and a small electric fan whirred on his desk. He said, "I don't know about you, but I'm looking forward to the rain we've been promised. Can't stand this clammy weather. . . . Sit down and tell me about Miss Scott. . . ."

Piper went over the story of his visit. The Superintendent listened and nodded from time to time and played with a pencil.

He pursed his mouth thoughtfully when Piper repeated the snatch of conversation he had overheard in the hall and described how he had seen Miss Reid and the good-looking man making love in the kitchen. When the story ended Mullett sat brooding in silence.

Eventually, he asked, "Have you any doubt about the gravity of Miss Scott's illness?"

"No, I checked with a friend who's a doctor. He confirms that she must be in a pretty bad way."

"And of course her husband must be aware that she hasn't long to live. . . . Wonder if this woman Reid knows it, too?"

"The conversation between them would indicate that she does," Piper said.

"Yes, I suppose so. Women are funny creatures, aren't they?"

"I haven't found much to amuse me in any of those that I've met so far in connection with the late Mr. Mitchell."

"You know what I meant," Mullett said. "Just think of the relationship between Miss Scott and this Joan Reid. If the old lady made a will leaving her the lot it means they got on pretty well. Miss Scott must still think a lot of her, for that matter, or she'd have changed her will when her wandering husband returned. Wouldn't she ? "

" She gave me the impression he blotted his copy-book a long time ago," Piper said. " If she had any regard for him at all she could alter her will now and leave him a share at least of the ten thousand Frank Mitchell left her."

Superintendent Mullett stared with faraway eyes at the window. When he looked at Piper again, he said, " Maybe she intends to give him a lump sum in cash before she dies. Saves a lot of death duty that way."

" That would be risky. She might die before the insurance company paid out."

" True. D'you think he knows the old lass has left everything to this Reid woman ? "

" I'm willing to bet on it. He's a good-looking fellow a bit younger than his wife and he could find someone better than her companion to have an *affaire* with."

" You think it's the money he's after ? "

" Well, it's more than possible. There was something about that passionate embrace in the kitchen which didn't impress me. It seemed a bit one-sided. She's not the type to make a man go crazy over her—especially a man with his looks and experience."

Mullett leaned back in his chair and nibbled the end of his pencil. At last, he said, " Bit of a lad is Mr. Alan Clark. After running around fancy-free for years he decides to go back to his wife and settle down. He comes across the envelope Frank Mitchell left with her, opens it and discovers that his ailing wife will inherit ten thousand pounds if she doesn't die before Frank does. So he arranges for Frank to die first. Dear, dear. . . ."

" It could be the explanation," Piper said.

" Most likely it is. Thomas Hood said : ' Evil is wrought by want of thought as well as want of heart. . . .' But if your theory is right, Clark must've thought this thing out very carefully."

" Calling it even a theory is too strong. It's just an idea that came into my mind when I saw what those two were up to in the kitchen. How you'd go about proving it is another thing."

" Depends where Mr. Clark was at eleven o'clock on Sunday night, July the ninth. Opens up an interesting field of inquiry . . . very interesting." The superintendent straightened himself and put down his pencil and asked, " Anything else you have in mind . . . or is that the lot ? "

" There's one thing more, but it has nothing to do with what I saw Clark and Miss Reid doing. It's only a vague idea at best. Now, what was the news you told me you had when I spoke to you on the phone ? "

" Ah, yes, you're entitled to your *quid pro quo*. . . . Well, while you were entertaining Miss Muriel Scott, I was similarly occupied with our friend Mrs. Mitchell. Only thing was "—the lines deepened in Mullett's face—" she didn't seem to find it at all entertaining."

" Why did you want to see her again ? "

" I didn't want to see her. I wanted her to see what we'd fished out of the Thames at lunch time yesterday."

" Frank Mitchell ? "

" Seems like it. He'd been carried down below Richmond Lock and the journey hadn't improved his appearance. Neither did the two young fellows who found him. Apparently they saw his body floating just beneath the surface and they used their oars to bring him closer to the boat. Knocked him about a bit in the process. Mind you, he was in a badly-decomposed condition and all ready to fall to pieces at the least touch. Ever seen anyone who's been in the water for any length of time ? "

" It isn't one of my favourite recollections," Piper said.

" No . . . always a nasty experience. Well, evidently he'd been lying in the mud of the river bed and, between one thing and another, he was in a somewhat messy state. The placid Mrs. Mitchell took one look at him, screamed bloody murder and fell down in a faint before I could catch her. We had quite a job bringing her round."

" I'm not surprised."

" I don't blame her, either. Although I'd tried to warn her what to expect she couldn't really anticipate what he'd look like. Corpses brought out of the river are always considerably bloated and a very bad colour when they've been in the water for a while. The little scavengers that live among the mud and silt of the river bed had been at work on him, too."

Piper said, " You don't like her, do you ? "

" In this job I can't afford either likes or dislikes. However, the way she reacted in the mortuary I'm pretty sure she'll have nightmares for some time to come." Mullett shrugged. " I wouldn't exactly say it was one of Alice Mitchell's best days."

" Did you have to take her to identify the body ? Wouldn't her brother have done just as well ? "

" I had an idea she might break down and talk if I could jolt her out of that phlegmatic calm of hers. Instead all I got was a first-class example of the good old Victorian swoon. Might've been due to a guilty conscience . . . on the other hand, might not. You've met the lady so your guess is as good as mine."

" I was just thinking of a quotation from Paradise Lost," Piper said. " You're fond of Shakespeare but there's one from Milton which might well apply to Mrs. Alice Mitchell."

Superintendent Mullett opened his eyes wide and laid his hands flat on the desk. He said, " I don't know Milton very well. Let's hear it."

" ' Now conscience wakes despair that slumbered, wakes the bitter memory of what he was, what is, and what must be.' "

" Ah, very apt, very apt, indeed. As so often happens, the sting is in the tail. ' . . . and what must be.' Those may be the operative words."

He linked his fingers together, propped his elbows on the desk and made a little rest for his chin. Then he added, " Right now I'd have been willing to bet that's what was scaring the wits out of her . . . but your story of the bit of nonsense between Clark and Miss Reid makes me not so sure."

" Have you had the pathologist's report yet ? "

" Received it a few minutes ago. Death was due to drowning. The coroner's been notified and I'm waiting to hear what time he'll hold the inquest."

" So Mrs. Mitchell will get her husband's death certificate without having to go to a lot of trouble," Piper said.

" What she won't get is the ten thousand pounds he left Miss Scott."

" That all depends on whether the second will is valid or not." Mullett seemed amused at the expression on Piper's face. " Be funny if the handsome Mr. Clark found he'd been making passionate love just for love . . . wouldn't it ? "

A phrase used by Miss Scott repeated itself in Piper's mind. " *If only my husband had been the steady type who knew how to stay out of trouble. . . .*" And either before or after his return she had made a will leaving all she possessed to Joan Reid.

. . . *At that time she almost certainly had no money—merely the house in which she lives and a few pieces of furniture. When he came back she didn't change her will . . . which means she didn't want him to get anything at all. She took him back but that was as much as she was prepared to do. There can't be much love between them. . . .*

Once again, Piper could hear her saying ". . . *I don't want Joan to have any trouble after I'm gone. I've left everything to her, you know, because of the way she looked after me. . . .*"

He said, " I've just thought of something."

Superintendent Mullett stroked his chin and made a puckered mouth. He said, " Yes ? "

" It struck me several times that Miss Scott wasn't always telling the truth—at least, not the whole truth. One of those times was when she told me her married life had been broken up because her husband was mostly away on some travelling job. Maybe it might be an idea if you got someone to check your files. What d'you say ? "

" Costs nothing to look," Mullett said. As he picked up the internal phone, he went on, " Something familiar about the name the moment you mentioned it to me. Can't quite place him, though. Never passed through my hands, that I'm sure of. . . ."

Into the phone, he said, " Hallo . . . give me Records, please. . . . Look, Superintendent Mullett here. Will you see if you've got anything on a man called Clark, Alan Clark, presumably spelled C-L-A-R-K. In his fifties possibly, and believed to be married. Wife was formerly a Miss Muriel Scott. . . . Right . . . I'll hold on. . . ."

As he waited he sat whistling under his breath, his heavy face thoughtful. Once, he glanced at Piper with the watchful, inquiring look in his eyes that stamped him unmistakably as a policeman.

Then the phone made little scratching noises and he picked up his pencil and scribbled *Alan Clark* on a scrap pad. He said, "Yes . . . yes . . . when was that? . . . I see. . . . Yes . . . Brighton Quarter Sessions . . . Canterbury. . . . How long did he get? Yes . . . go on. . . ."

The small voice in the phone went on talking while Mullett grunted and jotted down an occasional note. Then a look of wry surprise came into his face.

With his eyebrows pushed up, he said, "Did he, indeed? Serve him right, too. Teach him not to get ideas above his station. They say the shoemaker should stick to his last. That the lot? . . . No, thank you, not right now. . . ."

He slid the phone away and looked at Piper approvingly. "That was quite a hunch of yours. Our friend, Mr. Clark, has had three convictions: two for false pretences. His line has been talking foolish spinsters out of their savings on a promise of marriage. Most of them didn't fancy publicity, but eventually he was nicked. Got twelve months at Brighton Quarter Sessions. That should've been a lesson to him, but it wasn't. About eighteen months after he came out he was had up at Canterbury. This time the Recorder said he was a menace to the gullible women on whom he preyed. They were entitled to be protected from men of his type—three years."

Piper said, "And the third time?"

Superintendent Mullett glanced down at his notes and shook his head.

"There Mr. Clark made two mistakes. He embarked on a new racket . . . and he let himself get caught. Always a bad move for a crook to change his *modus operandi.*"

"What did he do?"

"Tried his hand at a pay-roll job. He and some other get-rich-quick merchant bashed a factory cashier when he was leaving the bank with the week's wages. Got away with over four thousand quid. The cashier was lucky to get away with his life. If he'd been hit just a little bit harder he wouldn't have lived to give evidence at the trial. Dangerous game, robbery with violence. You can finish up facing a murder charge."

"How long did they get?"

Mullett shook his head again. "We didn't manage to lay our hands on the other fellow. Clark had the dock all to himself. Refused to split on his pal and wouldn't help us recover any of the money. Got five years. The judge said he'd have been given a longer sentence only there was some doubt as to which of them had coshed the cashier. But if he got into any more trouble he'd get a lengthy spell of preventive detention."

Piper thought about Frank Mitchell and the Scotch terrier with its head battered in. He said, "When did Clark get out?"

"February of this year . . . apparently full of contrition for the wicked life he'd led and overflowing with honest promises that he'd go straight in future. The Prisoners' Aid Society fixed him up in a job with some driving tuition firm. Seems to have given no cause for complaint so far."

"I suppose the police have been keeping an eye on him?"

"For the first few weeks . . . yes. We'd have liked him to lead us to his pal. Not much chance of recovering the money after all this time; he'll have spent that long ago—"

"Or given it away," Piper said.

The superintendent leaned back and studied him reflectively. "What lies behind that cryptic remark?"

"You never discovered the identity of the other man," Piper said. "He could've been anybody . . . even a quiet, inoffensive and respectable citizen like Frank Albert Mitchell."

Mullett sat up very straight and rubbed his chin. He said, "You're certainly not lacking in ideas. . . ."

When he had studied his notes again, he said, "Let's take this one step at a time. You're suggesting that Mitchell and Clark did the job together; that Mitchell made Clark's wife an allowance out of the proceeds of the robbery . . . m-m-m?"

"Why not? Half the money belonged to Clark, anyway. And Mitchell—if it was Mitchell—owed Clark more than just money. After all, Clark might've got a lighter sentence if he'd betrayed his accomplice."

"True," Mullett said. "Very true."

He began playing with his pencil again as he went on, "Of course, this is all pure conjecture . . . but it's an intriguing thought. Assuming there's anything in it at all"—he tapped the end of his pencil on the desk to emphasise each word—"it's possible that the debt wasn't all on one side . . . m-m-m?"

"Meaning what?"

"There's something I haven't told you yet. According to Records it was an anonymous tip-off that led to Clark's arrest. Supposing—" Mullett stared up at Piper from under his brows—"supposing Clark had good reason to suspect that it was his partner who'd grassed?"

Piper said, "Then he'd have an even better motive for killing Mitchell. It might not have been loyalty that made him keep quiet at the trial. Maybe he was prepared to wait five years to pay back his side of the debt."

CHAPTER XIV

Mr. Charles Wheatley, Ll.B., was a tall thin man with a sour mouth and dyspeptic lines radiating from the corners of his nose. Greying hair fringed his bald head like a paper frill encircling some form of pink icing cake.

He cleared his throat affectedly several times before he said, " Most irregular, my dear sir, most irregular. You surely do not expect me to divulge the contents of the documents you refer to."

" I believe I know their contents already," Piper said. " All I'm asking from you is some idea as to their validity."

Wheatley sucked at his lips as though he had an unpleasant taste in his mouth. With his eyes on a point somewhere beyond Piper's head, he murmured, " I see. . . ." After further consideration, he said, " Perhaps you would be good enough to tell me again what your interest is in this, ah, matter ? "

" The late Frank Albert Mitchell was insured for a substantial sum with the Cresset Insurance Company. As we are both aware, the circumstances of his death were, to say the least of it, somewhat unusual. For that reason and also because of information brought to the attention of the company, it is felt that certain aspects of this claim should be further investigated. I have been retained by the company for that purpose."

When he had cleared his throat again, Mr. Wheatley repeated, " I see. . . ." He was still talking to the door behind Piper's back. " And you think the questions you are asking will help to clarify the position ? "

" I wouldn't ask them if I didn't think so," Piper said.

" One would hope not." He allowed himself a brief look at Piper's face before he said, " You believe you are acquainted with the terms of both these wills drawn up by the late Mr. Mitchell ? "

" That is so. Mrs. Mitchell gave me to understand that the original will left her husband's estate entirely to her. Miss Scott tells me she has handed to you a later will, prepared some time last year, in which she is named as a beneficiary to the extent of ten thousand pounds. Therefore you need not confirm these details if doing so would offend your code of professional etiquette."

" I certainly do not intend either to confirm or deny them," Wheatley said. When he had savoured the phrase, he repeated, " Either to confirm or deny. But—" he pointed a long pallid forefinger—" but I do not wish to send you away empty-handed. So I'm prepared to tell you this: if the later will was properly executed it most certainly cancels the former document."

" I appreciate that," Piper said. " What I am anxious to know is whether the later will was properly executed and if it will be granted probate. Apparently Mitchell had it drawn up by a solicitor other than yourself."

Mr. Wheatley seemed to think that the reference was in bad form. He said, " That is so." His eyes looked pained.

" Have you any idea why he should have acted in this way ? "

" None whatsoever."

" You handled all his other legal business right up to the time of his death ? "

" To the best of my knowledge—yes."

" He never gave you the impression at any time that he contemplated changing his will ? "

" We met very seldom . . . but the answer to your question is—no."

" Yet he employed another solicitor to draw up a fresh will. Strange, isn't it ? "

" Repetition of the fact won't provide us with his motive for so doing." Wheatley liked that phrase even better than the previous one. Judging by his tight-lipped smile he was academically amused.

Piper said, " Is it possible that this later will was not executed by Mr. Mitchell at all ? "

" Do you mean that someone might have forged his signature ? Quite absurd."

" Why is it absurd ? "

" Because I have examined both documents : the one that he signed here in this office and "—he made a sour mouth again—" the other which Miss Scott sent me. Without professing to be a handwriting expert I would say there's no question that both signatures are identical. I'm perfectly satisfied that Mr. Mitchell did, in fact, execute a later will for reasons best known to himself."

" What do you think would happen if Mrs. Mitchell chose to contest it ? "

" Oh, come now, Mr. ah, Piper, I am not the court. However "—he made a string of little husky noises in his throat—" I doubt if any action of that kind would succeed. After all, her husband left her adequately provided for . . . which, of course, is something I shouldn't tell you."

Piper said, " Thank you, Mr. Wheatley. I'm indebted to you for your courtesy."

" Not at all, my dear fellow, not at all. . . . I see from the papers that they've found the unfortunate man. Dreadful business, dreadful. One doesn't know what the world is coming to these days."

" There is a saying," Piper said, " that money is the root of all evil."

Wheatley said, " A misquotation, if you don't mind my saying so, a most common misquotation." He looked very pleased with himself as he took Piper's arm and gently shepherded him to the door.

There he added, " The correct version is : ' For the love of money is the root of all evil.' It occurs in the First Epistle of Paul the Apostle to Timothy ; chapter 6, verse 10. . . . You seem amused ? "

" Just a passing thought," Piper said. " You and Detective-Superintendent Mullett of Scotland Yard have quite a lot in common."

The later editions of the evening papers carried a report which caused Piper little surprise.

RICHMOND MURDER

The inquest on Frank Albert Mitchell has been postponed until July 27th because of illness of the dead man's widow. Mrs. Mitchell is understood to be suffering from shock following her identification of the body recovered from the Thames about two miles down river from the spot where Mr. Mitchell was murdered sixteen days ago.

A spokesman at Scotland Yard stated to-day that the police have received new information on the crime and they now believe they know the identity of the killer. Inquiries being pursued among the victim's former associates may lead to an early arrest.

On his way home that night Piper read the newspaper story again. He wondered who made up these statements issued to the Press. They were always carefully phrased to allow for almost any eventuality.

. . . Never does any harm to talk about prospects of an early arrest. Right now someone is probably getting very worried. The question is—who ? . . .

Alan Clark . . . or the demure Miss Reid who made passionate love to a dying woman's husband ? Mrs. Mitchell . . . or her brother James who was seen visiting the dead man's house not many minutes before the crime took place only a few hundred yards away ?

Or were the police chasing shadows ? Perhaps none of these people had brought about the death of Frank Mitchell. Perhaps he had been killed because his dog had annoyed a neighbour . . . or because someone had thought he was a Peeping Tom.

So many people might have had reason to kill the quiet inoffensive man who had lived with his quiet wife at Number 9 Douglas Crescent, Richmond. There had been quarrelling in that house. Mrs. Mitchell had been heard to say : "*. . . Mind your own business. . . .*"

Had she known that her husband was Alan Clark's

partner in a pay-roll robbery? Was it Mitchell who had been the anonymous informer?

If he had had no part in the crime for which Clark had been sent to prison for five years then all theories led back to a common starting point. He had been just a mild little shopkeeper who had made one big mistake. A man had to be able to trust the beneficiaries under his will before he put himself in a position where he was worth more dead than alive.

CHAPTER XV

THUNDERSTORMS BROKE over the Home Counties during the early evening. They travelled northwards in the next few hours, causing floods and some damage by lightning. By eight o'clock the storm-belt had spread over the Midlands.

James Newton disliked thunderstorms. He also disliked having his orderly life disorganised by last-minute changes in the duty rota. Both these aversions he voiced to a fellow-attendant called Reg Owen as the 4.05 from King's Cross to York rumbled its way north.

". . . Never done this run before. I was supposed to be on the 4.15 to Glasgow. . . . And all because I reported for work early they switched me on to this run. Said it would give them time to find a replacement for me on the 4.15."

"Too bad. Teach you not to be so conscientious next time. Still, York isn't a bad place. We're due in at 8.17 and if you haven't been there before you can do a spot of sight-seeing. It's an old Roman city, you know. Down in the foundations of one of the pubs there's a big circular bath that was used by the Roman soldiers over a thousand years ago. Lots of old medieval buildings, too, that're worth looking at."

"I'm not interested in either Roman baths or medieval buildings. The way it's getting dark long before it should, there'll probably be a storm by the time we arrive. When there's lightning about I get all creepy. Makes me feel as if my hair's standing on end. And it'll probably rain like the devil as well . . . so I'll be stuck in strange digs. . . ."

He was wrong about the rain. When they pulled into York, distant lightning flashed intermittently to the south and a growing mumble of thunder heralded the approaching storm, but no rain had yet fallen when he and Reg Owen left the station together.

Owen recommended a café in Friarsgate where he said there was generally cheerful company to be found. Newton thought he might give it a try. . . .

". . . Pity you've got a date. We could've spent a couple of hours together and you could've shown me the town. . . ."

After a brief conversation, they parted. The time was then twenty minutes to nine.

James Newton walked to his lodgings in Bishops Row, exchanged a few words with the landlady, and went up to his room. There he deposited his overnight bag containing a pair of pyjamas, a toothbrush and a tube of toothpaste, an electric razor, and a pair of socks.

Then he came downstairs. He told the landlady he had had something to eat on the train. ". . . I never have much of an appetite, anyway, in weather like this. Oppressive, isn't it ? Think I'll take a look round the town and try and get a breath of fresh air. Won't be late. . . ."

It was nearly half past nine when he left the house. By then premature darkness had fallen. There was frequent lightning and almost continuous thunder seemed to ring the old city with the roll of iron wheels.

At ten o'clock he visited the café that Reg Owen had recommended. Either because of the weather or for some unexplained reason the place was not very well patronised that night.

He commented on the fact that there were few customers to the Greek proprietor who served him with an iced orangeade. They passed a couple of idle remarks while Newton smoked a cigarette and complained about the weather. He spoke to no one else before he left ten minutes later.

The full violence of the storm broke not long afterwards. Long-awaited rain came down in a blinding cloudburst that cascaded from roofs, lashed the streets like hail, and caused gutters to overflow.

It lasted for nearly half an hour. Then the initial fury spent itself. By eleven o'clock quiet, steady rain was falling and the electrical storm had receded to the north.

There was minor flooding in several parts of the town. A house had been struck by lightning and set on fire. York had not known a storm of such severity for more than twenty years.

At eleven-thirty it was still raining—a soft, cool rain which seemed likely to continue for the rest of the night. The streets were empty, darkened windows glistening in the lamplight. Above the soaring spires of the Minster the sky was beginning to clear.

James Newton had not returned to his lodgings. After leaving the café in Friarsgate, he had walked along Goodramgate as far as the corner of Ogleforth. There his sightseeing tour came to an end.

A policeman on patrol found him lying in the shadow of a warehouse, his open mouth filled with rain, his head resting on a concrete step with blood congealing on the stone where he had apparently struck himself as he fell. He had been dead for some time.

CHAPTER XVI

MRS. ALICE MITCHELL received considerable publicity during the next two days. The popular Press extracted all they could from the story of a woman who had lost both husband and brother in violent circumstances within the space of little more than a fortnight.

She was photographed leaving the inquest proceedings in London . . . the crime reporter of one of the more sensational dailies interviewed her at the station as she was about to catch a train to York . . . there was another picture of her after the inquest on her brother.

It had been suggested to her that there was no real necessity for her to give evidence in his case: several fellow-employees were prepared to identify him. But she had insisted on making the trip north.

As one special correspondent put it ". . . The effect of this second bereavement shows itself plainly in her face. With the death of her brother she is now completely alone. She seems dazed and hardly able to appreciate what has happened. . . ."

Prominence was given to a report of the proceedings in York.

> . . . At the inquest this afternoon it was suggested that the deceased had probably stumbled and struck his head on a stone step.
>
> A pathologist, Dr. G. K. Humphreys, stated that he had examined the body and found no other sign of injury except a barely-perceptible bruise on the left shoulder. This could have been caused, in his opinion, when the deceased fell.
>
> A police witness stated that the spot where the dead man had been found was poorly lighted and it was quite conceivable that he had missed his footing.

The coroner, Mr. T. L. Watts, recorded a verdict of Death by Misadventure.

Piper read the story a second time after he arrived at his office the next morning. When he had disposed of his mail he stood looking out of the window at the dull, unsettled sky while he thought again about the coincidence of James Newton's death.

Coincidences happened every day. It could scarcely be anything else but an accident. Strange that it had taken place so soon after the murder of Frank Mitchell.

. . . He had been walking along a badly lit street . . . he had fallen and banged his head . . . and he had died. With that simple act he had eliminated himself from the list of murder suspects. . . .

If he had not reported early for duty, he would not have been switched to the 4.05 to York. If someone else had not failed to report for work there would have been no need to transfer Newton.

Links in a chain. . . . A fatalist would say that Newton was destined to die that night. The pieces were made to fit so that he was in York instead of Glasgow . . . to meet death in that place and at that hour. . . .

There was a light tap on the door. Without turning round, Piper said, " Come in."

He heard the door open. A familiar voice said, " I'm sorry to trouble you, Mr. Piper. I hope you won't mind me. . . ." The words evaporated as he turned to face her.

He said, " You're not troubling me at all, Mrs. Mitchell. Please sit down. You look very tired."

" I am tired. I seem to have no energy at all." She took a seat and adjusted her skirt very carefully as if afraid her underwear might show.

She looked the same as on that other day when she had been accompanied by her brother : same unbecoming green hat and black coat and black string gloves ; same pale, plump face and eyes that seemed to lack understanding.

When she had settled herself to her satisfaction, Piper

said, " I was sorry to hear about your brother, Mrs. Mitchell. You've been having a pretty rough time of it recently."

" Yes . . . yes, everything seems to have happened to me all at once." She folded her hands placidly on her lap and moistened her lips with the tip of a pale pink tongue. " That's why I've come to see you. Because now " —she glanced down while she tucked her feet under the chair and then she looked up at him dully—" I haven't really anyone else I can turn to. I felt I just had to talk to someone . . . and with Jim gone the only person I could think of. . . ."

" If I can help you at all," Piper said, " I'll be only too pleased. What is it you want to talk about ? "

" Well, it's about—my brother."

" Yes ? "

" I suppose "—she got rid of something that stuck in her throat and began again—" I suppose you've read about the inquest ? "

" Yes, I just finished reading the account a few minutes ago. Very unfortunate business. It's remarkable how accidents seem to happen."

Alice Mitchell looked at him in silence as though her mind were digesting his words one by one. Then she said, " That's just the trouble. It wasn't an accident."

Piper said, " All the evidence pointed that way according to what I read in the paper. What makes you think the verdict was wrong ? "

" I just know—that's all." She took a little shallow breath and repeated, " I just know."

" If you have any real reason to doubt the verdict, why not inform the police ? "

" They wouldn't believe me. It'd only be my word against—someone else's."

" Who is this other person ? "

" That Miss Scott—the one who talked Frank into making a new will."

" Are you suggesting that Miss Scott had something to do with your brother's death ? "

" Maybe she didn't do it herself but "—Mrs. Mitchell nodded solemnly—" she could've put somebody else up to it. She wouldn't let ten thousand pounds slip through her fingers."

"Do you mean your brother knew something that might've prevented her inheriting the money?"

"Oh, yes, he knew all right. That's why"—her voice broke—"that's why I know his death couldn't have been an accident. Him dying like that was just too convenient."

"Did he tell you what he'd found out?"

"Not exactly. But he said enough to make me feel pretty sure. . . ."

"When did you last see him?"

"The day he—he was sent to York instead of Glasgow." Her sudden weak anger was a childish emotion. "They should never have done that . . . they should never be allowed to do a thing like. . . ." She lost the trend of her thought and sat looking down at her gloved hands until Piper roused her again.

He said, "Distressing yourself over things like that won't do any good. What did your brother say to you that last time you saw him?"

Mrs. Mitchell needed time to rid herself of resentment. When at last she was able to concentrate on the question, she said, "Jim told me he'd been to Forest Hill . . . that's where she lives."

"Why did he go there?"

"He wanted to find out what kind of woman she was. Jim didn't believe"—something that could have been embarrassment showed fleetingly in her eyes—"that Frank would leave all that money to someone just because she'd been in service with his mother years and years ago. Jim thought there must be more in it than that . . . men being what they are."

"So he decided to pay Miss Scott a visit."

"Yes. He went on Wednesday morning. That was the day"—she looked down at her hands again and swallowed—"the day he was killed. . . ."

Piper could see no real grief in her empty face, no sign of any inner sorrow bravely borne. Within a matter of days tragedy had struck her a double blow. Any ordinary woman would have been red-eyed with crying, but there was no indication that she had wept at all.

. . . *She's no ordinary woman. Perhaps she's less than a woman in many ways.* . . . He said, " Did your brother speak to Miss Scott ? "

In a dull voice, Mrs. Mitchell said, " Yes, he spoke to her."

" Then he must've told you she's a very sick woman ? "

" So she makes out. I wouldn't be too sure myself."

" There isn't any doubt about it. I've seen her. She's suffering from an incurable disease and she's been told she hasn't very long to live."

" Maybe that's true, maybe it isn't. If it is true, why did she get Frank to leave her the money that should've been left to me ? "

" I don't think she used any undue influence on him. It seems to have been his own idea. Why he should have done so is not for me to say."

Mrs. Mitchell said, " No, but there's nothing to stop me saying it." Her sullen eyes had brightened as though she were now on sure ground. " It was Jim who put the thought into my mind."

" What thought ? "

" He spoke to that other woman—Miss Reid—and he said he didn't believe she was a companion or anything like that at all. Soon's he mentioned it, I remembered she wasn't bad-looking in a kind of way. . . ."

" I'm afraid you're not making yourself very clear, Mrs. Mitchell."

" It's clear enough to me. That young woman never was there as a companion. It was her my husband was keeping—not Miss Scott."

A nebulous thought took shape in Piper's mind. Alice Mitchell might be right. At least it was a possibility, a distinct possibility.

He said, " If there was anything at all in what you're saying, your husband wouldn't have left the money to Miss Scott."

Alice Mitchell drew in her small mouth. " That's easy to understand . . . if you appreciate how Miss Scott felt about Frank. She thought he was everything that's wonderful . . . judging by what she said to my brother. Jim was convinced the money was left to her so that it would be harder for me to contest the will than if I could say. . . ."

Her voice tapered off. She was no longer so sure of herself.

Piper said, " If we take your brother's idea a stage further, it means Miss Scott promised your husband that she would give the money to Miss Reid."

" Any reason why she shouldn't? My impression is that she'd have done anything Frank asked."

" But she's known for months that she can't live very long. Every expectation was that she'd predecease your husband. When she did, the will he'd drawn up in her favour would be worthless. Don't you see that? "

" I don't understand such things . . . but I don't believe Miss Scott was ill or thought she'd be likely to die soon at the time Frank made that will."

" Perhaps so. Nevertheless, she was considerably older than he was. They wouldn't expect that he'd die first, would they? "

" Somebody made sure he did," Mrs. Mitchell said. She knew which way she was going now.

" Would Miss Scott have anything to do with a thing like that if she thought the world of your husband? "

" Not Miss Scott, perhaps. There's somebody else I haven't told you about. When Jim visited the house he met a man called Clark. Nobody explained what Clark was doing there, but he didn't behave as if he was the lodger. . . ."

She moved her hands and then let them go still. " He told Jim that too many people were coming around asking questions. More or less ordered him out eventually."

" That doesn't prove anything."

" No, but from the way he spoke he was trying to hide something. And I think Jim discovered what it was. If I could prove it I'd go to the police. But it's no use doing that "—her eyes left Piper's face and travelled to the window—" now that Jim's dead."

He would have gambled every penny he possessed that she was a stupid, selfish woman. Probably she had never had an ounce of affection for anyone but her brother, and even his death had now obviously been pushed aside to make way for something that was, to her, of greater importance.

Piper said, " What could he have discovered ? "

She hunched herself slightly as she said, " I think he recognised this man Clark as somebody he'd seen near our house the night my husband was killed."

" But he didn't say that in so many words ? "

" No. It was just the way he spoke. . . . When he was leaving me that day he said he would do something about it soon as he got back from Glasgow . . . and that's all I know."

" It isn't very much," Piper said.

" Well, I thought it'd be enough for you to . . ." She stroked the back of her right hand and left him to complete the rest.

" Why me ? Why not tell the police about your brother's visit to Forest Hill on Wednesday morning and let them handle things ? Not that there's very much they can do in the circumstances. He wasn't assaulted in any way. He just fell and struck his head. It couldn't have been anything else but an accident."

" On the very day he'd been to her house and they knew he had his suspicions about them ? "

" You really think Clark had to silence your brother because he'd found out too much ? "

" Yes, I do."

" How did Clark know your brother would be going to York ? The trip was changed almost at the last minute."

" I don't know," Mrs. Mitchell said. Her eyes were becoming confused again. " Maybe he followed Jim after he left their house . . . and travelled to York on the same train. . . . You understand these things. I'm just a woman who's being robbed of money that belongs to her and. . . ."

. . . *All she cares about is money. It doesn't matter to her that she's lost her husband and her brother. She's prepared to drag Mitchell's name through the mire so long as she thinks it'll do her some good. . . .*

Piper said, " From what I'm told the second will is a perfectly valid document. Whether or not this man Clark had anything to do with your husband's murder, or was in some way responsible for the death of James Newton, has no bearing on the legacy that was left to Miss Scott."

Alice Mitchell brought her feet out from under the chair and stood up clumsily. In a bemused voice, she said, " I don't see how that can be. They talked my husband into leaving all that money to her . . . and then they killed him. All these years I've been allowed to think that whatever he left would be mine. I knew he must be insured although he never told me for how much. And now. . . ."

She stepped back a pace and shook her head in disbelief. " It isn't right . . . they can't do this to me. Because Frank made a fool of himself over some woman is no reason why I should be left . . ." She ran out of words there.

" I'm sorry," Piper said. " I'd like to help you, but I don't see what I can do. Unless it can be proved that Miss Scott entered into a conspiracy to cause your husband's death, she'll be entitled to inherit. The fact that he left such a legacy might, of course, have provided someone with a motive for his murder. It may help the police to lay their hands on the person who—"

He stopped at that point because Mrs. Mitchell was no longer listening. She had started walking backwards to the door with stiff little steps, her face peaky in childish anger, her eyes still bewildered.

As she reached for the doorknob, she said, " I don't care if they never find out who killed him. All I want is what I'm entitled to. I thought he was a fool . . . and all the time he was laughing at me behind my back. When I saw him lying on that table I told myself that's what he'd come to with his neat, fussy ways. . . ."

Piper said, " You're only upsetting yourself for no reason, Mrs. Mitchell. This won't do any good."

". . . He wouldn't have recognised himself . . . he was horrible to look at . . . just as he was horrible to live with. . . ."

"Mrs. Mitchell—please!"

". . . When he came home at night he ignored me. Once he'd put on his glasses to read the evening paper he paid no attention to me after that. . . . I suppose he thought he looked intellectual with those things on . . . people didn't know he only wore them when he wanted to make an impression on someone . . . always acted as if he was better than everybody else. . . ."

Her voice broke. She turned blindly and pulled the door open. Without looking round, she said, "It doesn't matter whether you tell people or not. I hated him. I should've killed him before he had time—"

She stopped and gave Piper a startled look over her shoulder. Then she went out and jerked the door shut. Her footsteps hurried along the corridor as though she were fleeing from something she had seen in Piper's face.

He sat for a long time thinking about the quiet house at Number 9 Douglas Crescent where Mr. and Mrs. Mitchell had lived their quiet lives. How could two people go on year after year keeping up appearances in the eyes of the world? There had to come a day when the façade of genteel respectability cracked and fell in pieces and exposed all their petty beastliness.

What kind of man had Frank Albert Mitchell been when she married him? How could he have ever thought he was in love with such a woman?

Perhaps they had been two of a kind. . . . In case some accident happened to him he had made sure that neither she nor her brother enjoyed the insurance money. That was mean—as mean as the woman he had deceived. . . .

He must have been in love with her in the years gone by or he would hardly have insured himself so heavily and made a will in her favour. It was only afterwards that he had learned to hate her as she hated him . . . until at last he had made sure she would never benefit if anything happened to him.

Why had he not left her when life at Number 9 Douglas Crescent became impossible? Why, in those last few months, had he not seen that he had now arranged his affairs in such a way that his own life might well become forfeit ?

. . . *Most men nurse some kind of secret during their lifetimes . . . it only remains a secret while they are alive. When a man dies the little pathetic facets of his life that he has tried so hard to keep hidden from the world become exposed.* . . .

What would happen to Mrs. Mitchell if it were ever proved that she had murdered her husband ? The defence could produce evidence of mental instability in the past, the fact that she had spent six months in a retreat. People would say she was more to be pitied than blamed.

. . . *So many women suffer from depression in middle life. When it gets too strong to be endured their minds become unbalanced. Often suicide presents itself as a means of escape. Some succeed in taking their own lives: some fail.* . . .

But what neurotic middle-aged woman resorted to murder ? Alice Mitchell had indulged in a lot of wild talk. She was stupid and greedy and cunning, but she was not the type to batter her husband to death. At the very worst, poison might have been the weapon she would have used : not a heavy walking stick to club the life out of him. Violence was inconsistent.

Piper remembered something she had said that was also inconsistent. He got up and walked about the office while he tried to reconcile two things that contradicted each other.

One was a fact, the other a statement made by her. Therefore she must have been lying. Yet there seemed to be just no reason why she should lie. The remark had not been important and it had merely slipped out. . . .

He went back to his desk, dialled the Cresset Insurance Company and asked to be put through to the general manager.

". . . Mr. Burrows ? Piper here. About this Frank Mitchell case."

" Oh, yes. I see his brother-in-law went and got himself killed, too. Wonder how much he was insured for ? "

" According to what came out at the inquest his death was an accident."

" You can't always go by that . . . as you know only

too well. However, our only interest is in Mitchell. Made any progress ?"

"Well, I know more now than I did when I started. One thing that's come to light is that he made a new will some time last year in which he bequeathed ten thousand pounds to some woman who acted as nanny to the family when he was a child."

"Interesting. . . . Must've given his widow quite a shock. In less than three weeks she's lost husband, brother, and ten thousand pounds. No wonder the papers said she looked dazed."

"It's the money I want to talk about. Whatever excuse you have to make, don't pay the claim on any account."

"Going to be difficult to withhold payment. We'll have to give some reason. I believe a solicitor called Wheatley's already been in touch with us. He wants to list the assets of the estate so that he can apply for probate . . . and this policy is the biggest single item."

"I know that. But it doesn't matter what you have to say or do: postpone the actual payment as long as you possibly can."

"We won't be able to stave it off indefinitely, you know. Still, I'll do my best. What's behind all this ?"

"I don't want Miss Muriel Scott, chief beneficiary under Mitchell's will, to inherit the money he left her."

"Why ?"

"Because she might go thc same way as he did," Piper said.

Within a few minutes he made a second phone call. Detective-Superintendent Mullett was out, but he was able to speak to Sergeant Pugh. From Pugh he obtained the address of a young man called Kenneth Smart.

While he put his papers away and prepared to go out he made up his mind on one thing: if young Smart and his girl-friend both gave the same answer, then Alice Mitchell was lying. There could be no other explanation.

Yet she had had no reason to lie, no reason at all even to say such a thing. It had been nothing more than the petty spite of a stupid, resentful woman.

But. . . . Even a spiteful remark had to be based on some foundation of fact. It had come out spontaneously. What could have prompted her to make such a sneering comment unless it were based on the truth ? And if it were. . . .

An elusive thought came and went in Piper's mind. It posed an absurdity. Or was it so absurd ?

CHAPTER XVII

Kenneth Smart was an ordinary young man with smooth brushed-back hair, a pleasant face, and an air of honesty. He repeated his story in a straightforward manner and seemed to have no difficulty recalling the exact details of what he had seen and heard that night.

". . . No, there was no one following the man with the dog. It was pretty quiet and I'd have been able to hear if somebody'd been behind him on the path."

" What if they'd walked on the grass ? "

" Wouldn't have made much difference. Besides, I'd have seen them . . . same as I saw him when he went past."

" Wasn't it too dark at that time of night ? "

" Well, it never gets really dark there on a fine night like that. I recognised him when he got close enough."

" Of course, you'd seen him several times before ? "

" Oh, yes. Any evening Betty and I were there we'd be sure to see him taking his little Scotch terrier for a walk. Regular as clockwork, he was. We could tell what time it was almost to the minute when he went by."

" Did you notice if he looked back at all ? "

" As far as I remember he just walked straight on."

" Was he near enough for you to see the expression on his face ? "

Kenneth was puzzled by that question. He said, " Well, not really. But he looked the same as he'd always done. Behaved the same way, too. Had a habit of slapping the dog-chain against his leg . . . and he walked with his shoulders back and swung his arms. Wore a light cap and sometimes an open-necked shirt. I've always thought a man of his age who wears heavy-rimmed spectacles doesn't look quite right without a tie . . . if you know what I mean."

Piper said, " I know what you mean. He loses a certain amount of dignity by trying to look too youthful . . . is that it ? "

" Yes. Of course, in hot weather I suppose people don't worry too much about looking dignified. Besides, it was late, anyway, and he was only taking the dog for a walk."

" Where was the dog ? Running ahead of him ? "

" No, it was a well-trained little thing. Always kept to heel. Damn' shame it had to die like that. Wonder what kind of person could do such a trick ? "

" I wonder," Piper said. " Now, tell me : after Mitchell cried out, how long was it before you heard the sound of him falling into the river ? "

" Not long. Maybe a quarter of a minute . . . or even less."

" Did you run to see what was happening as soon as the trouble began ? "

" Almost at once."

" But before you reached the spot you heard someone running away."

" Yes. They weren't very far ahead of me, at that."

" Could you tell if they were a man's footsteps—or a woman's ? "

" I wouldn't like to say. It was just someone running. Everything happening suddenly like that got me a bit confused. Besides I was paying more attention to the noise of him floundering about in the water."

" So the person who ran off could have been either a man or a woman ? "

" I suppose so . . . although I can't see a woman being able to do a thing like that."

" Is it possible that the person who ran away didn't go very far ? I mean did the footsteps go farther and farther off or did they stop before they'd gone any distance ? "

Kenneth gave the question careful thought. At last, he

said, " It's a bit difficult to say definitely. You see, by that time Betty had come chasing after me and between us we made quite a bit of noise ourselves. After that, the poor devil in the water took all our attention. As it was I wasted too much time or I might've saved him."

" You can't blame yourself for that. Where was he when you and Betty pushed through the bushes ? "

" By the time we got to the edge of the bank he was maybe twelve or fifteen yards out and just about level with where we were standing. The current was carrying him downstream pretty fast and he went under almost at once."

" Was everything quiet after that ? "

" For a couple of seconds. Then Betty started begging me to take her home. Next thing I knew, I nearly fell over the body of the Scotch terrier."

" During those few seconds after you saw Mitchell drown was there any sound at all of the person you'd heard running away ? "

" No. Now I come to think of it, that's what scared Betty stiff. She told me afterwards she felt all the time that somebody not far away was watching her. I said it was just imagination. Now "—he moved uncomfortably—" I'm not so sure."

" Neither am I," Piper said. " Do you mind if I have a chat with Betty ? "

" Not at all . . . if you think it'll help."

" She might remember something you've forgotten."

" Then it's all right with me . . . although it'd be a lot better if she wasn't reminded of it. D'you want to go and see her right now ? "

" Before the day is over, anyway."

" All right. I'll give you her address. But she won't be home until after six."

" That's all to the good," Piper said. " It'll give me time to take a walk beside the river and have a look at the spot where it happened. . . ."

At five o'clock the sun had gone in and a freshening breeze came off the water. On the opposite bank a man with a megaphone was running along the towpath exhorting a crew of four to greater effort.

In the channel between the towpath and Eel Pie Island people were taking afternoon tea on the deck of a motor launch to a background of gramophone music. As Piper walked along the north bank he could see children playing cricket in the sports ground between Orleans Road and Lebanon Park.

Soon he came to the place that Kenneth had described. Here was where he and Betty had lain and whispered to each other in the dusk. Beyond the next bend would be the spot where there was a clump of bushes. . . .

. . . No more than two hundred yards away. If a young man sprinted he could reach there in less than a quarter of a minute even in the dark. . . .

The grass had grown again in the little clearing, but he could still see where someone had used a sickle close to the bushes screening the spot from the footpath. In a sheltered nook partly overhung by branches there was the little mound near which the police had found Cynthia Blake's powder compact. From the river bank to the surface of the water was a drop of about four feet.

He stood and listened to the river slapping against some partly submerged rocks while he built up a picture in his mind of those moments when Kenneth and Betty watched Frank Mitchell's final struggle before he went under.

Somewhere out of sight the fleeing footsteps had come to a halt. The question was—why? Once the job was done what reason could there have been to delay making an escape? Was it to make sure Mitchell was dead?

That would mean he had not been intended to fall into the Thames. Such a thing had been unforeseen. It introduced a risk that had not been allowed for—the risk that he would be rescued and live to talk. . . .

. . . So someone made off but didn't go too far away. Someone waited and listened over there in the dark until Kenneth and Betty had gone. Perhaps that same someone then came back here and made sure Frank Mitchell was safely disposed of. There would be plenty of time to get away —plenty of time before Kenneth notified the police.

It had evidently been well planned but badly executed: vicious and stupid . . . like Alice Mitchell. . . .

She said she had not known that her husband was heavily insured. Judging by her look of surprise when she heard the amount she had been telling the truth. But looks were often deceptive.

He walked aimlessly here and there for another few minutes, thinking about Miss Reid with her arms round Alan Clark's neck, the look of death on Miss Scott's face. Then he made his way through the bushes and went back along the footpath towards Orleans Road.

Mrs. Willcock was a small, fussy woman who evidently assumed that every man who looked like a policeman must necessarily be one. Piper allowed her to go on thinking so. It saved explanations and avoided the possibility that she might refuse to let him speak to her daughter.

After Betty joined them in the over-furnished room they called "the lounge," Mrs. Willcock stayed as a silent protective audience. When she thought Piper was not looking she took off her pinafore and stuffed it under a cushion.

Betty confirmed almost detail for detail Kenneth Smart's account of what had happened.

. . . No, she had not heard anyone go by before Mr. Mitchell came along. He always passed that spot at the same time. . . .

"How long had you been there?"

"From about nine o'clock."

"And he passed you about eleven. . . . Did you hear sounds of anything unusual during those two hours?"

"No. A few people came along the path before it got dark, but they were just ordinary couples. I could hear them talking and laughing."

"You didn't hear anyone who appeared to be alone?"

"Not that I remember. Of course, I wasn't paying much attention." She seemed to regret the added remark when she noticed that her mother had turned to look at her. With a trace of embarrassment in her voice, she said, "I've already told all this to the gentlemen who came to see me. They asked me to let them know if I remembered anything else . . . but there's been nothing I could think of."

" I'm just checking one or two points," Piper said. " After Mr. Mitchell had gone past how long would you say it was before his dog started to bark ? "

" Oh, about a minute or so."

" Until he shouted : ' No . . . no, keep away . . .' had there been any sound of conversation ? "

" Nothing at all. Of course, I probably wouldn't have heard them if they'd been speaking quietly."

" Probably not. Now, tell me this, Miss Willcock. Although it was practically dark, you say you recognised him as soon as he came close enough. Was that because of the way he was dressed or the fact that he was accompanied by a little dog or what ? "

" Well, mostly because of the way he was dressed . . . and his build . . . and things like that. . . ."

" I see. Go on."

" He always wore a light-coloured cap and those glasses that've got thick rims. I could always tell who it was, too, even before I saw him because of the way he swung that dog-chain as he walked."

" So you could hear him coming when he was still quite a little way off ? "

" Yes, it's very quiet there at eleven o'clock at night."

" Of course, it must be. A man would be easily recognised by the fact that he was carrying a dog-chain and wearing a light cap . . . wouldn't he ? "

Betty Willcock knew what Piper meant. After a little uneasy glance at her mother, she said, " You think someone was waiting there all the time ? "

" That seems the obvious conclusion. Did he show any sign that he noticed you ? "

" No, he just walked straight on . . . like he always did."

" And that's how it happened," Piper said. " He wore a cap that made him easily recognisable, and the rattling dog-chain let people know he was approaching. Above all it was his regular habit to take the same walk at the same time night after night. . . . Thank you, Miss Willcock, I think that's about all. . . ."

Betty and her mother saw him to the door. Mrs. Willcock said, " I hope you don't mind me saying this . . . but I think it's about time my daughter was allowed to forget this whole nasty business. Wouldn't you say she's been asked enough questions ? "

Piper said, " I certainly would. And I can promise you that I won't trouble either you or your daughter again. . . ."

He walked back to the footpath along the river bank and timed the journey at a normal walking pace from the little clearing to the foot of Douglas Crescent. Then he went on to Richmond station and caught a train back to town.

If he was right, Alice Mitchell had lied. And one thing he now knew. He could no longer delay paying a return visit to the home of Miss Muriel Scott.

CHAPTER XVIII

By HALF-PAST EIGHT a gusty wind was blowing and it was trying to rain. The first spattered drops speckled the pavement as he went up the flagged path and rang the bell.

It was the good-looking man who opened the door. The knot of his tie had slipped down and his iron-grey hair needed combing. In a disgruntled voice, he said, " Yes ? "

Piper said, " Mr. Clark ? "

" That's me. What d'you want ? "

" My name's Piper. I represent the Cresset Insurance Company. I was here the other day."

" Were you ? So what ? "

" Well, I'd like to speak to Miss Scott again . . . if I may."

Clark said, " So far as I'm concerned, you may not." His eyes travelled down to Piper's feet and back up to his face before he went on, " I don't believe you represent any insurance company. I think you're a copper. Even if you aren't, my wife's had enough visitors to keep her going for quite a long time."

"Including James Newton," Piper said.

Nothing changed in Clark's face. He said, "Who told you he was here?"

"His sister."

"Did she also tell you I offered to throw him out if he didn't leave?"

"Yes, she did. She mentioned at the same time that that same night he fell and banged his head—and died. I think you ought to know that she's saying some pretty wild things, Mr. Clark."

"Such as what?"

"She doesn't believe Newton's death was an accident."

"Is that what you've come to tell my wife?"

"No. There's something else I'd like to discuss with her."

There was no inflexion in Clark's voice as he asked, "What is this something else?"

"I'd rather not go into that with anyone but Miss Scott personally," Piper said.

Clark put his hand on the edge of the door and narrowed the gap a few inches. He said, "You may, or may not, be an insurance representative . . . I don't know and I don't much care. What I do know is that we've had enough discussions and questions to last me a long time. First it was you, then Newton, and after that a couple of busies kept popping in and out of here so that the house is beginning to get a bad name. Well"—he closed the door a little more—"I'm having none of it . . . see?"

"Must be quite embarrassing," Piper said. "But I promise you I won't take up much of your wife's time. All I want is to—"

From the room on the left of the hall, Miss Scott's reedy voice called out, "Who is it, Alan? Why are you standing arguing at the front door?"

Clark said, "Nothing for you to bother about."

"But who is it?"

"Haven't you been disturbed enough in the last few days?"

" Do you mean someone from the police is here again ? "

" No, it's a man called Piper. He says he's from the Cresset Insurance Company. I've told him—"

" Don't you tell him anything. If he wants to see me, let him come in. You're certainly not going to keep him standing outside in the street."

With a shrug, Clark pulled the door wide open. He said, " I suppose you know what you're doing. . . ."

As Piper went past him he added, " Go on in. You heard her." Then he closed the door sharply and went stiff-legged across the hall and into the kitchen.

Miss Scott was sitting hunched-up in the chair near the window. She looked even more shrivelled than on his previous visit. Except for the glitter of her sunken eyes, the slight pulsing of a vein in the cords of her neck, she had the look of a corpse.

She said, " Come in, Mr. Piper, come in. I've been hoping I'd see you again. Pull up a chair. . . . That's right."

There was no strength in her voice. She sounded as if the slightest effort exhausted her.

Piper said, " I wouldn't have troubled you, but I'm hoping you may be able to help me."

" I'll be glad to . . . if I can. You're much nicer to talk to than the man who was here from Scotland Yard."

" Who was that ? "

" I think he said his name was Mullett, Superintendent Mullett. Do you know him ? "

" Yes, we've met. From the way your husband spoke just now, I gather that the Superintendent rubbed him the wrong way."

She plucked at her wrinkled bony fingers and sighed. " My husband hasn't got much time for anyone connected with the police. You see "—she drew a little difficult breath and closed her eyes momentarily as though in pain —" he's been in prison."

" I know," Piper said.

" Oh, you do ? " She nodded slowly and went on nodding as though she had forgotten to stop. Then she said, " You can't blame Alan for feeling as he does. He says the police never let a man alone once he has a criminal record."

"All depends on the kind of life he chooses to live when he comes out of prison," Piper said. "But I didn't really come here to talk about your husband, Miss Scott. At least, not until we've discussed something else. I'd like to ask you one or two questions about Mrs. Mitchell."

"What can I tell you about her? All I know is the little that Frank told me. You've met her, you've spoken to her. . . ."

With shaking hands, Miss Scott felt for the handkerchief in her sleeve, dabbed her pallid mouth, and put the handkerchief away again. "Whatever I've heard hasn't been to her credit . . . but now you'll think I'm being cross with you . . . and I'm not." She tried to smile and failed. "You understand, don't you?"

Piper said, "Of course. Please don't upset yourself. This is just something that puzzles me. And it isn't so much to do with Mrs. Mitchell as her husband. He wore spectacles, didn't he?"

Miss Scott moved awkwardly and rested her head against the back of the chair. She said, "Yes, he did . . . for many years. He always had a tendency to be short-sighted right from the time he was just a little boy."

"Did he have to wear glasses all the time?"

Something that could have been a new awareness came into Miss Scott's deep-sunk eyes. She said, "Why d'you ask?"

"Well, two people say he was wearing glasses the night he was attacked. That is confirmed by the fact that his broken spectacles were found beside his cap and walking stick—and the body of his dog. Yet. . . ."

"Yes, Mr. Piper? Go on." It could hardly have been alarm that had troubled Miss Scott. Now she was merely curious.

"His wife says he wore glasses only for reading . . . and even that was something in the nature of an affectation."

"Oh, I see. She still hates him, doesn't she?"

"I think she must've hated him for a long time," Piper said.

"Yes . . . I didn't believe Frank, but he was right. She's the kind of woman"—Miss Scott closed her eyes for a moment and rubbed one dry, dead hand up and down the back of the other—"who can destroy a man. Frank would've made her a good husband . . . if she'd only let him. But she was too wrapped up in herself and that brother of hers."

Piper said, "Now that her brother's gone her sole concern is Frank Mitchell's insurance money. However, I'd like to settle this point about the spectacles. Did he wear them all the time?"

"Well, quite a lot of the time. He had them on frequently when he came to see me. Of course"—she moved again as though trying to find a more comfortable position—"I have seen him without them."

"But they weren't merely an affectation . . . or necessary only for reading?"

"Frank didn't have any affectations," Miss Scott said.

"Then it looks as if Mrs. Mitchell was lying. Question is—why?"

"Alice Mitchell doesn't need to have a reason. She'll say anything that comes into her head so long as it shows Frank up in a bad light. Hate is motive enough for her."

"But why should she have hated him so much?"

"Who knows? Perhaps it was because he was superior to her in every way. She's semi-illiterate and she lacks imagination . . . and I doubt if she's mentally more than about twelve years of age. There never were two people who had less in common."

"Yet he married her," Piper said.

For an endless moment Miss Scott stared at him, her shrunken face bleak with all the sorrow in the world. Then she said, "I've never told anyone this before . . . but it doesn't matter now. She tricked Frank into marriage. It wasn't true . . . but he believed her."

. . . The old, old story. . . . How often is it kept buried out of sight so that no one ever knows? No one would ever have known in this case if Frank Mitchell had not taken a walk along the river bank on a quiet summer's evening as darkness fell. . . .

Miss Scott said, " Funny, isn't it? He was the one who was tricked, yet she did all the hating. If she'd known he was heavily insured, I believe she could've killed him."

. . . *This is the moment. If you don't grasp your opportunity now it may never come again.* . . . Piper said, " Given the courage, she might've murdered her husband . . . but she could never have harmed her own brother. And someone killed him, Miss Scott."

The yellow, wrinkled hands lying on her lap began to tremble. She went on looking at Piper while she swallowed several times before she managed to say in a smothered voice, " No . . . I don't believe that. She's made you think so because she's got a warped mind. She hates everyone and everything that's been connected with Frank. They proved at the inquest that it had been accidental."

He could hear Alice Mitchell saying ". . . *I know his death couldn't have been an accident. Him dying like that was just too convenient.* . . ."

There was no room in this affair for coincidence. . . . Piper said, " The jury based their verdict on the evidence submitted to them. They didn't know that James Newton visited you on the morning of the day he died: they didn't know he spoke to your husband: finally, they didn't know what he discovered while he was in this house."

In an uncertain voice, Miss Scott asked, " What did he discover? "

" That your husband has known the contents of Frank Mitchell's will for a long time . . . and he's always been under the impression that whatever you inherited would come to him."

She closed her eyes and sat breathing shallow breaths in and out of her open mouth. All the bones of her face showed through the skin.

At last her eyes opened wearily and she said, " I should've known you wouldn't let kindness stand in the way of your duty. When the police came they asked my husband the questions you're going to ask me. I don't know what answers he gave them . . . but they went away. I'm too tired to go on fighting, I haven't the strength to protect him any more, as he wants me to do. I've forgiven him time and time again . . . but it's been no use. Now, I've no time left."

Piper said, " Where was your husband on Wednesday night ? "

" I don't know."

" Where did he tell the police he'd been ? "

" Here . . . at home."

" Did they ask him about that Sunday night out at Richmond ? "

" Yes."

" What did he say ? "

" The same thing. He'd spent the evening with me."

" Was that true ? "

Almost inaudibly, Miss Scott said, " No."

" Since the police were here have you asked him where he did spend that Sunday evening ? "

" Yes. He said he sat in here reading until very late."

" Is he in the habit of doing that kind of thing ? "

" I don't know. I go to bed early."

" If it were true, why should he need you to tell lies about it ? "

" He says a man with his record doesn't stand a chance once the police get their hands on him."

" Do you believe that's his only reason for asking you to provide him with a fake alibi ? "

She took a long time to answer. With empty eyes she sat pulling at her fingers until she reached a decision.

Then she looked squarely at Piper and said, " I owe my husband nothing . . . and Frank Mitchell everything. I won't shelter Alan any longer. He's entitled to pay for what he's done."

" You know that the law can't make you testify against him, don't you ? "

" The law won't need me to testify," Miss Scott said. She put both hands on the arms of her chair and pulled herself upright. In a dry voice, she went on, " When I read that the dog had torn a piece out of somebody's trousers I went and got out Alan's old flannels. Then I examined the rest of his clothes . . . and I found he'd been trying to remove a stain from one of his jackets."

" What kind of stain ? "

" It looked like blood," Miss Scott said. Her hands were trembling again. " It was a dirty mark on the cuff of one sleeve. When I went to his wardrobe again a day or two later, the stain was almost gone. He must've been working on it between times."

Far back in Piper's mind, a voice seemed to be saying, ". . . *She hasn't long to live. With the end only a few months off at the most, she couldn't possibly have anything to gain . . . and you might be wrong. The whole thing's absurd. But you're being paid by the Cresset and it'll cost them ten thousand pounds. Which comes first—your integrity . . . or sentiment for a dying woman ? Why should you feel sorry for her, anyway ? . . .*"

He said, " What about the torn flannel trousers ? "

" I cut the buttons off them, then I buried them in the heart of a smudge fire that the people next-door left smouldering at the foot of their garden one night."

" Why didn't you do the same thing with his jacket ? "

" I've had no opportunity. The neighbours haven't burned any more garden rubbish . . . and in warm weather we don't light the kitchen stove." Her hands were shaking, but now there was resignation in her face.

" Didn't he miss the pair of trousers ? "

" He never mentioned anything about them to me."

" Probably too scared," Piper said. " Now, Miss Scott, what do you propose to do about all this ? "

She fondled one dry, wrinkled hand in the other while she went on looking at him. Then she said, " I thought you might tell me what to do."

" It isn't my problem. After all, he's your husband."

She seemed to shrink smaller still. In a different voice, she said, " Not the kind of husband he should've been. He left me before he was sent to prison when he found out I wouldn't go on supplying him with money. That was all he had wanted me for."

" But he came back when he learned you were ill."

" That wasn't his reason. He came back because he had nowhere else to go."

" The last time I was here you told me he'd been good to you."

" What else could I say ? I hoped then . . ." She sighed. " Now, I've nothing left to hope for. I know now that he's been making a pretence of kindness because he thought I'd be bound to leave everything I've got to him. During these past few months he's known I can't last long . . . so it's obvious what he's been doing."

" Doesn't he know you've made a will in favour of Miss Reid ? "

" We've never talked about wills. Even Joan herself doesn't know."

. . . *Wonder what she'd say if I told her about that scene in the kitchen ? Don't suppose it would make any difference. The only danger now is if he finds out she won't back up his alibi for that Sunday night. He'll get rid of the jacket . . . and he'll get rid of her. There'll be no other course open to him. She doesn't realise the dangerous situation she's got herself into. But if I do what she wants things may work out right. . . .*

Piper said, " Are you sure the jacket's still there ? "

Miss Scott sucked in her lips and glanced nervously towards the door. " Yes. I looked in his wardrobe last night when he was out of the house. He must've been cleaning that stain again . . . it's almost gone. You can hardly see it."

There was only one decision that Piper could make. He said, " We've gone too far to go back now, Miss Scott. You leave me no alternative but to inform the police. Is that what you want ? "

Her eyes fixed themselves on his as though trying to read his thoughts. He told himself there was still time . . . but who was he to condemn her after what he had seen in the kitchen ?

Then she said, " I've known all along that it had to come. Alan has had his chances time and time again. This time what he's done is unforgivable. Do what you have to do."

" I won't question you any more," Piper said. " You can leave me to do the rest."

Her skeleton hands took a hold on the arms of the chair

and she pulled herself forward as he stood up. In a stronger voice, she said, " If you hadn't come this evening, I'd have had to do it myself. Tell the police they'll find evidence here that my husband murdered Frank Mitchell."

CHAPTER XIX

A SEARCH through Alan Clark's wardrobe produced a check sports jacket with a mark on one sleeve that appeared to have been caused by some cleaning fluid. When asked for an explanation he admitted there had been a stain on the sleeve and volunteered the information that he had removed it with lighter fuel.

. . . No, he was unable to account for the stain. He'd probably got it through leaning on some café table. It was just a stain . . . could've been from soup . . . could've been from anything wet and sticky. What did they think it'd been—blood ?

Detective-Superintendent Mullett said, " That, in the circumstances, is a most unfortunate suggestion—coming from you."

Further questioning provided no further answers. Clark was unable to account for the whereabouts of a pair of grey flannel trousers which he admitted having once owned.

. . . They had been an old pair . . . it was a long time since he last remembered wearing them . . . no, he had not thought to ask where they had gone. . . . If he had missed them at all he would have assumed that someone had sold them to a rag-and-bone man. . . .

After a further examination of the jacket, Superintendent Mullett said, " I shall have to retain possession of this garment. You will be given a receipt for it, of course. I should also like you to accompany me to Scotland Yard for the purpose of making a statement. Have you any objection to doing so ? "

Alan Clark said, " Why should I have any objection ? I know the procedure as well as you do. Either I go willingly, or you'll cook up some charge and pull me in on a warrant."

"From which I gather that you'll come quietly—to coin a phrase . . . m-m-m ? "

"Why not ? Costs me nothing. I've told you the truth. Being a copper you don't recognise it even when it's stuck under your nose. One thing, though, you'd better get into your head before we go any further. . . ."

"Yes ? "

"I had nothing whatever to do with what happened at Richmond. Neither you nor anyone else can prove I killed that fellow Mitchell."

"So far, no one's suggested any such thing," Mullett said. "If you go on like this you may talk yourself into serious trouble."

"And that would break your heart, wouldn't it ? "

The superintendent looked at him coldly and then shrugged. "Trouble with you, Clark, is that you're a fool. If you hadn't been a fool you wouldn't have spent all those years in prison."

"Maybe. But you're not putting me back there on some trumped-up charge."

Mullett said, "There's one thing I'm going to tell you that obviously you won't believe. I'm only concerned with getting at the facts. Personally, I don't care whether you spend the rest of your life in gaol or not. If it weren't for the fact that I'm a patient man, you'd be under arrest right now."

Tests conducted by the forensic laboratory revealed that the stain had been caused by human blood some of which had penetrated to the underside of the cloth. There was a second stain on the sleeve lining just inside the cuff. From this a solution was prepared for a blood group check.

Clark was asked to wait until the results of the tests were known. He voiced no objection when he was also asked to furnish a sample of his own blood.

At eleven-thirty that night Superintendent Mullett received the lab. report. It stated that the bloodstains on the jacket belonged to group O. This was the same group as Frank Mitchell's blood. Clark belonged to group A.

He was brought back to Mullett's office and told that the stain on his sleeve was human blood. Then he was asked if he could account for its presence there.

By now he was unable to pretend that he was not seriously worried. He said the only explanation he could think of was that he must have cut himself at some time or other without knowing it.

Superintendent Mullett asked him if he would like to reconsider his answer in the light of the fact that the blood on his jacket had been checked against his own and found to belong to a different group. Therefore it must have come from some other person. Could he explain that ?

Clark remained silent and looked frightened. After two or three false starts, he said, " Don't beat about the bush. There's something else . . . isn't there ? "

" Yes. Laboratory tests prove that the bloodstains on your sleeve belong to the same group as Frank Mitchell's. Would you care to explain how that comes about ? "

In that moment, Alan Clark aged far beyond his years. With stupefaction in his voice, he said, " It isn't possible . . . it just isn't possible."

" You'd better face the situation," Mullett said. " It's not only possible, it's absolute fact. And you're the only one who can explain how that blood got there."

" But it can't be his blood. This is just "—he put a hand to his head and looked round the room as though seeking a way of escape—" just fantastic."

" Why can't it be ? "

" Because I never laid a finger on Mitchell. I've had enough trouble in my life. When I came out this last time I made up my mind it would be the last time : I was determined to go straight. I was nowhere near Richmond that night."

" Are you sure ? "

" Of course I'm sure ! What good would it do me to try and kid you ? "

" No good at all, I'm afraid. Now, since you know so

positively where you weren't that night, you must remember equally clearly where you were. Why not tell me and we'll get the whole thing settled here and now ? "

Clark must have been expecting the question, but he was still unable to hide his confusion. The answer tumbled out too hastily. " I told you the last time you asked me that. I was at home all evening."

" Alone ? "

He hesitated and his eyes betrayed him. A little too loudly, he said, " You don't need to ask that, either. You know I was with my wife."

" I don't know anything of the kind," Mullett said. " She says she went to bed about nine o'clock, as is her usual custom. After that she has no knowledge at all of what you did. You might've remained at home for the rest of the evening . . . or you might've gone out."

" I didn't go out. I sat and read until very late and then I went to bed." He was lying and not very convincingly.

Superintendent Mullett asked himself how a man of such transparent weakness could have induced so many women to make fools of themselves. He had a veneer of good looks and an air of virility . . . and that was all.

. . . *Strange how women nearly always succumb to the things that're weak in a man. . . . They can resist strength . . . maybe because they resent it. But that protective mother-instinct swamps all their judgment when they sense a man's inner weakness. He's just a little boy to be coddled. . . .*

With someone like Clark the odds were that bluff would succeed. Mullett said, " What would you say if I told you that someone saw you leaving the house that night ? "

In the same over-loud voice, Clark said, " I've been around too long to fall for an old stunt like that. You can't produce anyone who saw me go out."

" Can't I ? "

" No, you can't."

" Then why did you ask your wife to say you'd spent the entire evening with her when that wasn't true ? "

" Because "—he stumbled over the word and glanced round with a hunted look in his eyes—" because I know what you busies are like. A man doesn't stand a dog's chance if he's been inside. You've got to pin the murder of Frank Mitchell on somebody—and I'm nice and handy. It'll save all of you a lot of trouble if I—"

"Don't talk rubbish! You had another reason for asking your wife to provide you with an alibi. You don't want anyone to find out where you really were that night. Isn't that the case?"

After a struggle with himself, Clark said, "I didn't kill Mitchell . . . I wasn't anywhere near Richmond. No one can prove I had anything to do with it."

"Be a bit awkward for you if somebody saw you there," Mullett said.

"That won't work, either. You haven't got any fake witness. That fellow Newton is dead."

"Indeed?" Superintendent Mullett interlaced his fingers to make a prop for his chin. When he had studied Clark thoughtfully from under his brows, he asked, "How did you know I was talking about James Newton?"

Clark shifted uneasily and cleared his throat before he said, "My wife was told—something about him."

"Who told her?"

"A man called Piper . . . from the Cresset Insurance Company."

"Who put the idea into his head?"

"I believe it was Mrs. Mitchell."

"Just like the House that Jack Built," Mullett said. "If you weren't at Richmond that Sunday night, Newton couldn't have seen you . . . so he couldn't have given his sister the impression that he did; therefore she's wrong to plant such a suspicion in Mr. Piper's mind; and he's equally wrong passing it on to your wife. Yet the remarkable thing is. . . ."

When he could bear the strain of waiting no longer, Clark asked, "What's remarkable?"

"Your wife evidently believes that Newton did see you at Richmond on the night Frank Mitchell was murdered."

"I tell you I wasn't there." Traces of sweat were beginning to show on Clark's face.

"All right. Let's assume that's true. But you weren't

at home, either. Wouldn't you be wise to tell me where you really were ? "

After he had cleared his throat with difficulty, Clark said, " Whatever I say, you won't believe me . . . so I'm not saying any more. Now you can do what you like."

Superintendent Mullett made a little grunt of disgust. He said, " Like every crook I've had the misfortune to meet, you're a fool. You're afraid to tell the truth because you think it'll incriminate you. How you can be so stupid as to believe that lies will get you out of the mess you're in, beats me."

He stood up and flapped a hand in dismissal. " Go home and sleep on it. Maybe a night's rest'll put some sense into that thick head of yours."

Alan Clark got up from his chair and fumbled with his hat. While he stared at the superintendent in disbelief, he said, " I don't understand. . . . You mean—you're not arresting me ? "

" Do you think I ought to ? "

" No, but—"

" Then go home," Mullett told him. " And stay where I can find you. If you try to do a bunk I'll have you inside . . . make no mistake about that."

When he reached the door Clark looked back and said, " There's a catch in this somewhere. You think you'll trick me into saying or doing something . . . don't you ? Letting me go like this is a trick. I know how the police work."

Mullett said, " What you're trying to say was much better expressed a long time ago in the phrase : *Timeo Daneos et dona ferentes*, which means, for your information, ' Beware of the Greeks when they come bearing gifts.' On the other hand, there's an old adage about not looking a gift horse in the mouth. Now, get out."

Clark said, " I'm going. The quicker I get out of here the better it'll suit me."

He had the door open when Mullett said, " Just one thing. . . ."

" Well ? "

" I hope for your sake "—the Superintendent's voice

developed a sudden bite—" that nothing happens to your wife in the near future. Take good care of her, very good care of her. . . ."

Piper heard his phone ringing as he unlocked the office door. He went in and threw his hat on a chair and picked up the receiver.

An uncertain voice said, " Oh, Mr. Piper . . . this is Kenneth Smart. You remember what we talked about yesterday ? "

" Yes."

" Well, I've just thought of something. It might not mean much and I don't want to waste your time. . . ."

" You're not wasting my time. Go ahead."

" Well, when I was thinking over what happened that night I remembered one thing that hadn't struck me before. When Betty and I reached the clearing behind those bushes and ran to the river's edge, Mitchell was just about level with the spot where we were standing. We had time to get a quick glimpse of him before he went under. You see what I mean, don't you ? "

" I certainly do," Piper said. " And thanks very much for ringing me. I should've thought of that myself. You've helped to crystallise something that's been worrying me since I was out at Richmond yesterday."

" Now, it's worrying me," Kenneth said. " I wish you'd tell me what it means."

Piper said, " A certain lady I know should be able to explain much better than I can. If the explanation is what I think it is, you're going to get a little surprise."

" What kind of surprise ? "

" A pleasant one," Piper said, " The Cresset Insurance Company will probably want to show their appreciation of the help you've just given me. . . ."

He phoned Detective-Superintendent Mullett and asked for an appointment. Mullett said he had been about to suggest the same thing . . . and how would it be if they met in his office at a quarter to ten ? . . . .

From the window of his room on the third floor there

was a view of scudding clouds through which a watery sun showed itself at intervals. Down below on the oily Thames a tramp steamer slowly beat its way upriver against the drag of the current. Across the water County Hall bulked grey against the smoky sky.

Piper accepted a cigarette and a light and listened to an account of the interview with Alan Clark. When it came to an end, he said, " I don't blame a man in his position for being puzzled. Why didn't you arrest him ? "

Mullett smiled and doodled on his scrap-pad with a newly sharpened pencil. When he had drawn a flight of steps with what looked like a guillotine at the top, he said, " Before I make a pinch I like to be reasonably sure that the charge will stick. In this case I'm not so sure."

" Why ? "

" Because Clark had plenty of time to get rid of that jacket . . . but he didn't. He must've known the dog had torn a lump out of his trousers, yet he left them for his wife to find. All very curious, isn't it ? "

" Maybe he didn't think he'd ever be connected with the affair."

" He knows too much of police methods to rely on that. The fact that Mitchell's later will left a tidy sum of money to Miss Scott had to come out before she could inherit. Clark would realise it was inevitable that we would then turn our attention to the occupants of a certain house in Forest Hill."

" You could be crediting him with too much foresight."

" Possibly," Mullett said. He added a tiny figure to his drawing of a guillotine at the top of a flight of steps. " Tell me this : what was it first made you suspect that Clark had a motive, although his wife told you she'd left everything to her companion ? "

" The fact that he was in the habit of making love to Miss Reid."

" Didn't you tell me you had a feeling it was the other way round ? That she might've been making love to him ? "

" Yes. But does that make much difference ? "

The superintendent smiled again and sketched another

figure at the top of the steps. While he studied it with his head on one side, he said, " It might make a very big difference. Supposing she staged that love scene because she heard you coming out of Miss Scott's room and expected that you'd take a peek in at the kitchen door to see what was going on between her and Clark ? "

" Why should she do that ? "

" To show you that Clark had a motive for the murder of Frank Mitchell. If Miss Reid was in love with him he'd soon be able to get his hands on a packet of money whenever his wife died . . . if Mitchell died first."

Piper said, " But, in that case, she could only want to throw suspicion on Clark so as to make sure no one would suspect her."

" Exactly," Mullett said. A third figure had taken its place in front of the guillotine. This one was lying down with its head on the block.

" That's all very well," Piper said. " But none of it accounts for the bloodstains you found on Clark's jacket."

" True."

" If he didn't do it, how did he get Mitchell's blood on his sleeve ? "

" The quiet Miss Reid might have the answers to a few questions like that."

" Someone else could've known they'd been having an *affaire*," Piper said. " Maybe I wasn't the first one to catch them making love."

The superintendent put down his pencil and stared into the middle distance. After a time, he said, " She's supposed to have loved Mitchell as if he'd been her own son. You'd never get a jury to believe she could bring herself to murder him because he'd left her a lot of money in his will . . . especially when she's got only a few months to live."

" If you believe her story," Piper said.

Mullett nodded as though his own thoughts had been confirmed. " Don't you ? "

" I don't believe any one of them in this whole business. From the very start everybody's told lies—including Alice Mitchell."

"Oh. . . . I was wondering"—Mullett poked among the oddments in a glass tray on his desk and picked out a small piece of rubber—"when that lady's name would crop up." As he began erasing the knife of the guillotine, he added, "Did you have anything particular in mind?"

"No. I've just come to the conclusion that I wouldn't trust a single thing she's ever said."

Superintendent Mullett put the rubber back in the glass tray and used his pencil to draw the knife in the dropped position. Now the little recumbent figure was minus its head.

In a reflective voice, he said, "You might not be far wrong at that. From information I received just before you phoned me, I'd say she wasn't a very trustworthy person: information, I may add, that didn't really surprise me. In view of your energetic efforts in this business"—he seemed to be mildly amused—"I think I'm entitled to tell you what I learned this morning."

"About Mrs. Mitchell?"

"Yes, about Mrs. Alice Mitchell. That faint of hers in the mortuary the other day might've been genuine enough, but her identification wasn't." Mullett's tone changed. "The man we fished out of the Thames wasn't her husband."

Piper remembered the words she had used: ". . . *He wouldn't have recognised himself . . . because he was horrible to look at . . . just as he was horrible to live with. . . .*"

Any woman might well have had a faint when confronted with a body that was already beginning to look less than human. Remorse need not have had anything to do with it.

Piper said, "She'd have identified anyone at all as her husband so long as she thought it would make sure that the whole thing was over and done with. All she worried about was having him disposed of officially."

"That's my opinion, too," Mullett said. He glanced at the sketch on his pad and smiled grimly as he went on, "I've had my doubts about her all along . . . and this morning they were confirmed."

"How?"

"I got a report that someone had come forward and

said he had reason to believe the dead man might be his father. Seems the father was a retired architect who lived alone at Staines since the death of his wife and who'd had a nervous breakdown. Recently he'd been suffering from the delusion that he was going blind. . . ."

The superintendent opened one of the folders lying on his blotting pad and took out a closely-typed sheet of foolscap. "According to this, he got worse as time went on. In the past month or so he became something of a recluse and wanted nothing to do with his family because they kept telling him it was all imagination. Yesterday his son suddenly realised that no one had seen anything of him for some time . . . so he decided to pay a call."

Mullett ran his finger down the page, line by line, while he murmured, ". . . This doesn't particularly interest us . . . there's a bit farther on . . . ah, here we are. . . ."

He propped his elbows on the desk and read aloud in a flat voice: "'. . . I found the house locked up . . . the milkman said there had been a note telling him not to deliver until further notice. . . . No one living nearby had seen anything of him for the past couple of weeks or more. I had a terrible feeling that he might have done something—pretty bad. So I went to the police. . . .'"

Piper said, "Did he give them a positive identification?"

"Oh, yes. He mentioned some distinguishing marks before they took him to view the body. His father had a large mole in the hollow of the throat and he'd broken the little finger of his left hand a number of years ago. The bone hadn't been properly set so he was left with a slight deformity."

"And those marks were on the body?"

"Sure, it was his father all right." Mullett closed the folder, gave it a light pat, and leaned back in his chair. "Cleared up that end of the business just in time, too. I had started to think I might've been misjudging Mrs. Alice Mitchell."

"Why hadn't you believed it was her husband's body?"

Superintendent Mullett smiled lazily and shook his head. When he had stretched himself, he said, "If I tell you that I'll lose a little bet I've made with that friend of yours,

Inspector Hoyle. He's staked half a dollar that you know all the answers."

"Hoyle flatters me," Piper said. "All I've managed to do so far is collect a lot of annoying questions."

"Such as?"

"One of them you've just answered when you told me it wasn't Frank Mitchell's body . . . although his wife said it was."

"Where does the knowledge take you?"

"Now that I know you haven't found him yet, it confirms my impression that she's lied about everything."

Mullett said, "'The love that in a woman's eyes doth lie . . . and lies . . . and lies. . . .'" His lop-sided smile matched the grimness of his voice.

"They say that love and hate are never far apart," Piper said. "Perhaps it'll only be by chance that Mitchell will ever be found."

"You think so?"

"Yes. I think the Thames will keep its secret . . . unless the person who helped to dispose of him chooses to talk."

"Do you know who this person was?"

"I believe I could make a guess."

"But you're not sure?"

"No one can be sure of anything in this affair," Piper said. "Otherwise you'd have charged Clark with the murder of Frank Mitchell."

"Maybe I will before very long."

"Before you do, find out first if he's ever been a blood donor."

"Why?"

Piper said, "That's something I'd like to keep for another time. But I'll leave you with a thought which might provide the answer: certain kinds of love can destroy just as surely as hate."

"Cryptic," Mullett said. His eyes were bright with a new alertness.

"Not if you think about it. Then you'll know why everybody has lied since that Sunday night when Mitchell took his last walk with Alexander along the banks of the river. Out of all the lies we may be able to reconstruct what happened."

Superintendent Mullett nodded. He waited until Piper got to his feet and then he pointed to a small framed card hanging on the wall alongside the door.

He said, "I keep that thing there to console me whenever I feel sorry that fate chose me to be a policeman. It says: Great is Truth and It Shall Prevail. Nice thought, wouldn't you say?"

"I'm not sure," Piper said. "There are times when people might be better off not knowing the truth. This could be one of them. Good morning, Superintendent. . . ."

CHAPTER XX

THE BELL at the other end went on ringing for a long time. Piper leaned against the wall of the call-box and listened to the rhythmic burr-burr . . . burr-burr . . . burr-burr . . . while he rehearsed in his mind what he was going to say.

If she denied it he could do nothing. There was no proof. . . .

Then Miss Scott's thin reedy voice said, "Yes?"

Piper said, "I didn't expect you to answer the phone. Isn't your husband there? Or Miss Reid?"

In a tone she had never used before, Miss Scott said, "No . . . I'm alone."

"I wanted to speak to Mr. Clark. When will he be back?"

"He won't be coming back. He's gone."

"You mean—he's left for good?"

"Yes. I didn't think he'd want to go on living here after what had happened . . ."

"After what you tried to do to him," Piper said.

She made a little sound that could have been the start of a protest. Then she became silent. At the other end of the line there was a faroff noise that could have been made by someone knocking at a door. Piper thought he could hear other voices, a muffled bump that might have been a door shutting.

After that there was no sound except a faint humming on the line until Miss Scott said, " Whatever I did was nothing compared with what he did to me."

" In your eyes perhaps you felt justified," Piper said. " But other people won't see it that way. The fact that he betrayed you once again by having an *affaire* with Miss Reid gave you no right to plant faked evidence against him."

" Why do you say it was faked ? Why should you believe him and not me ? I can't understand how the police came to let him go. When they took him away I thought . . ." She ran short of breath and she was unable to go on.

" You thought the bloodstains on his jacket would be enough to condemn him," Piper said. " But if your husband had murdered Frank Mitchell he would've disposed of that jacket. He wouldn't have been such a fool as to leave it in his wardrobe for anyone to find."

Very faint and far away, Miss Scott asked, " Do the police think the same as you do ? Is that why they let him go ? "

" In the circumstances they couldn't arrest him . . . not while they had reason to believe that you might've wanted to punish him for betraying you. It'll save a lot of unnecessary trouble if you admit it now. You see that, don't you ? "

Except for little fleeting noises on the line the phone remained silent. Piper asked, " Are you there ? "

She mumbled something indistinct. Then she said, " I wasn't interested in punishing him. I only wanted to protect Joan so she wouldn't make a fool of herself over him like all those other women did. If I'd told her what he was she wouldn't have believed me. She's a sweet girl . . . and she's been good to me. I felt I had to protect her. This was the only way."

" Whose blood did you use to make the stains on his jacket ? "

After another short silence, Miss Scott said, " My own."

" How did you know it belonged to the same group as Frank Mitchell's ? "

" When Frank was only a little boy he fell off his bicycle one day and was quite badly hurt. He lost a lot of blood . . . and they used me to give him a transfusion because they said I was the same group." In a different voice, she added, " I've always liked to think that he had some of my blood in him. Somehow, after that, it seemed to make us belong to each other. But I don't suppose you can understand how I've always felt towards him."

" I think I do understand," Piper said. " Did you know your husband's blood belonged to a different group ? "

" Yes. He used to be a donor many years ago. . . . The idea came to me when I found out about him and—Joan. I knew he wasn't in love, really in love, with her. It was just that he knew about the will I'd made."

" Wouldn't you have cared otherwise ? "

" Why should I care ? It won't be very long now before he'll be free to do as he likes. If he'd been the right kind of man who could've made Joan happy, I'd have been pleased for both their sakes. But all he was after was the money he thought she was going to inherit."

" Seems almost a pity you didn't succeed in having him convicted of murder," Piper said.

In a stronger voice, Miss Scott said, " Oh, but I did succeed in another direction. When he came home late last night after the police let him go he said he couldn't live here any more. . . . I'd tried to get him into trouble. Obviously I must've been thinking there was something between him and Joan. So he was leaving to show me how wrong I'd been."

" Did Miss Reid deny it, too ? "

" Yes. What else could she do ? I told them I didn't mind if they were really in love with each other. When I was gone I'd like to think they'd get married . . . so long as he wouldn't marry her just for the sake of any money she might be left. To make sure his feelings were the right kind, I was going to change my will so that she'd get practically nothing. That way he'd have to work to keep his wife . . . for a change."

" What did he say to that ? "

" He lost his temper. In less than a minute he let Joan see him in his true colours. I'd never have believed he could forget himself so completely. Of course, he'd had a bad fright when the police were questioning him."

" So he and Miss Reid didn't go away together ? "

" No. She had her eyes opened properly. If—" Miss Scott's voice faltered—" if I don't change my will she'll be quite safe now."

Piper said, " Presuming that your husband was only after the ten thousand pounds, Miss Reid's been quite safe all along. You see, the Cresset Insurance Company won't pay out on Frank Mitchell's policy."

Miss Scott's breath seemed to catch in her throat. When she recovered, she asked huskily, " Why shouldn't they pay ? Tell me : why shouldn't they pay ? "

" Because I've advised them not to do so."

" But why . . . why ? "

" I don't think you really need me to answer that," Piper said. " I know who ran away from that spot on the river bank at Richmond. I also know the part you played in the disposal of Frank Mitchell."

The phone made a choking sound. Then there was a noise as though she had dropped the receiver. Then there was nothing.

He said, " Hallo . . . are you there ? Hallo. . . ."

A moment later he realised he was talking to himself. The line was dead. And to ring her again would merely be a waste of time.

It took him two or three minutes to pick up a taxi. As he gave the driver the address of the house in Forest Hill, pity for Miss Scott crowded out all his other emotions.

He had to knock several times before at last he heard dragging footsteps cross the hall from the room on the left. There was some fumbling with the lock . . . little sounds of distress. Then the door opened.

Miss Scott said, " Oh, it's you. . . . I thought it was —someone else."

She was breathing with difficulty from the exertion and

she had to hold on to the edge of the door with both hands to support herself. The yellow skin of her face seemed almost transparent.

" I wanted to make sure you were all right," Piper told her.

She stood looking at him, the breath wheezing in and out of her slack mouth : a stooped old woman who was not really old, but whose years had run out. Then, with resignation in her eyes and her voice, she said, " You'd better come in . . . you'd better come in."

As she let go of the door and shuffled round she nearly fell. Piper caught her just in time.

He had to help her into the room on the left and almost lift her into the big, high-backed chair in which she always sat. After she was safely settled, he went out and closed the front door.

She opened her tired eyes when he came back into the room. Very faintly, she said, " I shouldn't have hung up on you. It was rude of me . . . but I didn't feel well. There seemed nothing more for us to talk about, anyway."

" Someone called here while we were speaking on the phone," Piper said. " That was why you hung up."

For a moment she seemed prepared to deny it : but only for a moment. Then she said, " There's no reason why I shouldn't tell you. It was her—Frank's wife."

" What did she want ? "

" A little chat—a friendly little chat. At least, that's what she called it."

" A chat about what ? "

" Money. She's got no other interest in life. She wanted me to refuse to take the legacy that Frank left me in his will."

" Didn't you tell her the insurance company won't pay out ? "

Miss Scott said, " No." While she fumbled for the handkerchief in her sleeve, she added, " I don't believe they can do a thing like that."

" It's true, nevertheless. You'll never get any money out of the Cresset Insurance Company."

"That's what you say. They're bound by law to pay out."

"Would you risk going to law . . . in view of what I know?"

"You know nothing," Miss Scott said. "All you've been trying to do is—"

Pain gripped her suddenly. With her eyes tightly shut she sat gulping air noisily as if there was not enough to breathe, her fingers twisting and tugging at the handkerchief.

Piper walked over to the window and turned his back on her. Now that the time had come he had no stomach for what lay ahead.

Outside on the close-trimmed lawn a flock of starlings disputed over some crusts. In the drive of the adjoining house a small boy in a blue buster suit pretended that his tricycle was a racing car. Somewhere across the street a door banged shut with every gust of wind.

He waited for a long time until at last Miss Scott said in a weak voice, "Mr. Piper . . . I wonder. . . ."

"Yes?"

"There's some brandy in the top drawer of that desk. Would you get it for me? It helps—sometimes."

"Of course."

He found the small flask and brought it to her. "Shall I get you a glass?"

"No . . . no, I'll manage all right—this way."

She plucked at the cap until it came off and fell unheeded on to the floor. Then she put the flask to her lips and let brandy trickle into her mouth. It was only with an effort that she forced herself to swallow it.

Gradually her breathing slackened. The pounding of the big vein in her neck became less pronounced.

With the flask held between her hands, she looked up at him and murmured, "It's gone. . . . Thank you for being so kind."

"My being here is no kindness," Piper said. "If you insist on claiming Frank Mitchell's life assurance, I shall be obliged to tell the company what I know."

Miss Scott took a tiny sip of brandy and sucked her

bloodless lips while she went on staring at him. Her eyes were a little brighter.

She said, " You don't know anything, Mr. Piper. You only think you know. There's nothing you could prove."

Piper said, " That remains to be seen. Meantime, I'm interested in your chat with Mrs. Mitchell. What was the outcome ? "

" I agreed to let her have half the money."

" You had no need to do that. Whose idea was it ? "

" Call it a compromise, if you like."

" In other words, you came to terms because you had to."

With her eyes on the flask of brandy, Miss Scott said, " No . . . no, I decided it was the only proper thing to do. After all, she was his wife."

" That wasn't your reason," Piper said. " I thought I was the only one, but evidently Alice Mitchell's found out, too, and the price of her silence is five thousand pounds. Am I right ? "

" Why don't you ask her ? "

" I'd be wasting my time. Tell me this instead : did Mitchell take part in the robbery for which your husband got five years ? "

She looked momentarily startled. With no deceit in her voice, she asked, " Whatever gave you that idea ? Frank never had anything to do with my husband."

" Then who was the other man ? "

" Someone called—" She stopped and shook her head. " Never mind. He was caught not long afterwards and sent to prison for some other offence. He's still there."

" What about the money they stole when they attacked that cashier outside the bank ? "

" Alan hid it in a safe place before he was arrested." She smiled faintly. " At least, he thought it was a safe place."

" Wasn't it there when he came out of prison ? "

" No." She smiled again. " I distributed it anonymously among a number of children's charities."

" What did he say when he discovered the money wasn't where he'd hidden it ? "

" He guessed I was responsible. When he asked me about it I told him what I'd done."

" How did he take that ? "

" Quite well. I realise now "—her smile faded—" that he hoped to get it back, with interest, when I left my money to Joan Reid."

" Did he know he might never have been arrested if someone hadn't informed on him ? "

" No, I don't think so." She stroked the flask and gave Piper a long straight look. " If he'd asked about that I'd have told him I was the informer."

" Why did you do it ? "

" Because if he hadn't been caught and punished he'd have done it again . . . and again. That first time he'd used violence, the cashier nearly died. Sooner or later, he'd have killed someone. I still thought there was a chance of saving him, a chance that he might learn his lesson so that we could build some kind of married life together. Then a week or two ago "—she shook her head and sighed—" I found out that he could never change."

" So you decided he should be put away where he could do no further harm for a long time," Piper said. " Where was he the night of that business at Richmond ? "

Without expression, Miss Scott said, " I can only guess that he took Joan somewhere . . . maybe a room in some hotel."

" Which would've made things look even worse for him if it became known. There's still a possibility that he may be charged with the murder of Frank Mitchell."

In the same toneless voice, she said, " Is there ? " She seemed more interested in finding the cap of the brandy flask.

Piper handed it to her and said, " I'd like you to know I think you're a very clever woman, Miss Scott."

" Do you ? " She fussed with the metal cap and then laid the flask on the arm of her chair before she asked, " Why ? "

" Because you wanted your husband to be tried for Frank's murder. When the defence called you to give evidence on his behalf you'd have confessed that you put the bloodstains on his jacket because you were jealous of his association with Joan Reid . . . and she'd have sworn that he was with her at eleven o'clock that Sunday night. Between her testimony and yours, I doubt if any jury would ever have convicted him."

Miss Scott nodded and rubbed her dry hands together. With no emotion in her eyes, she asked, " What good would all that do ? "

" A man can't be tried twice for the same offence," Piper said. " Alan Clark would've been acquitted. So far as the police were concerned he was guilty, but he'd got away with it. So. . . ."

" Yes, Mr. Piper ? " Her hands were becoming restless.

" No further inquiries would be pursued. The police file on the case would be closed. When all the excitement was over we'd have another unsolved murder—officially. Everybody would be sure you and Miss Reid had lied in the witness box to save your husband . . . but they could do nothing about it."

She closed one hand over the other. When she had swallowed several times, she said, " I've already told you why I put bloodstains on his jacket. If the police do arrest him, I can promise you I'll deny any knowledge of it." In a sharper voice, she asked, " How do you know he didn't kill Frank, anyway ? "

" Because Mitchell's body hasn't been recovered yet," Piper said. " Of course, you won't have heard about it, but the man they found in the Thames the other day has now been identified as someone else."

Her eyes began to burn. She was trembling all over. With difficulty, she said, " I don't want to hear any more. Please go away."

Piper said, " All right, Miss Scott, I'll go. But it won't make any difference. The Cresset Insurance Company won't pay. If you sue them, they'll see that the case drags on until—I'm sorry to have to say this—until you're dead. So, whatever you do, you must lose."

The pulse began beating sluggishly in her stringy throat and the cords of her neck stood out when she swallowed again. It took time before she found the words she wanted.

At last, she said, " I was wrong about you . . . and I don't know what you mean."

" You know only too well. The point now is that the police must be told. Will you tell them . . . or shall I ? "

Almost inaudibly, Miss Scott mumbled, " Tell them what ? "

" That no one murdered Frank Mitchell," Piper said.

Her eyes sank deeper in her head and she seemed to stop breathing. For endless seconds she sat staring at him, mute and trembling, until eventually she said in a lifeless voice, " You're guessing . . . that's all . . . you're guessing. You can't prove anything."

" Does it make any difference ? The only thing which matters is that all your scheming and planning has been for nothing. There will be no claim made on the Cresset Insurance Company. And for that you have only yourself to blame."

While her hands twisted on her lap, she said, " What did I do wrong ? I tried so hard . . . I tried so hard. It was all for him. . . . How could it be my fault ? "

" Merely because you tried too hard. You gilded the lily. If you hadn't faked the evidence against your husband, I'd never have suspected that you might've taken part in an attempt to defraud the insurance company. What you did focused attention on yourself. It hardened the doubts I've had for some time now."

She put both hands over her face and began rocking to and fro. In a thin wailing voice, she said, " I did it for the best . . . I only wanted to make sure. . . . Oh, dear . . . oh, dear . . . oh, dear. . . . I did it for him . . . I wanted nothing . . . it was all for him. . . ."

" Escape from his wife and with ten thousand pounds to start all over again," Piper said. " That was enough to tempt a man like Frank Mitchell to fake his own death."

Miss Scott took her hands from her face and looked up at him with tears filling her eyes. She said, " It was her brother who ruined everything. If he hadn't gone to York. . . . Frank was safe there. No one knew him . . . no one would ever have suspected. . . . And then that man Newton had to bump into him. . . ."

Piper said, " And that was when something which had started out with the killing of a dog turned into murder."

" No, no, that isn't true ! Frank didn't do anything like that. It was an accident. Newton threatened he'd expose the whole thing if he didn't get a share of the money. Frank had to agree. There was no other way out."

" Except to shut James Newton's mouth," Piper said.

Miss Scott beat her withered hands together and made a string of little whimpering sounds in her throat. She said, " Oh, please, you mustn't think that ! Newton did it all himself. He caught hold of Frank and threatened him with what would happen if he didn't keep his bargain. Frank tried to make him let go . . . and Newton tripped and fell. . . ."

" Whether it was accident or murder is not my problem," Piper said. " But how do you know what happened, anyway ? "

She closed her eyes and took a long breath before she looked at him again. She said, " Frank told me."

" When ? "

" This morning . . . after you spoke to me on the phone. Alice Mitchell had just gone."

" You mean he came here ? "

" Yes. He couldn't stay away any longer. He had to talk to me . . . he had to explain—about Newton. As if I could ever think he'd do a thing like that. . . ." Her pale smile came and went briefly.

" He killed the dog," Piper said. " You'd better hope there are no dog owners on the jury when he's charged with causing Newton's death."

After a long silence, Miss Scott said, " He was so sure that nothing could go wrong. It looked more genuine this way than suicide. We couldn't afford any delay. . . . I haven't got much time left."

" You'd have collected the money on the policy and handed it over to him when the fuss had died down. In another few months it would've been too late for anyone to question what you'd done with it."

" Yes. It couldn't fail. That's what he impressed on me—it couldn't fail. But it seems that—" A spasm of pain stopped her saying any more. The big blue vein was throbbing in her throat.

Piper said, " You forgot to take one thing into account. The river flows quite fast at Richmond. A semi-conscious man should've been carried at least a short distance down-river by the time that young couple reached the spot. That is, if he'd entered the water there. Yet he was still level with the place where it happened when they saw him go under. Once that thought took shape, the rest wasn't difficult to understand. I guessed that he must've thrown a heavy stone into the water, run a few yards upriver along the bank so that people would hear someone apparently escaping, and then he slipped quietly into the water and let the current carry him past the spot where the attack was supposed to have taken place. Isn't that right ? "

She nodded and went on nodding while she murmured, " You'd have had nothing but your suspicions. There was no proof it wasn't what it seemed to be. But she remembered they'd once spent a holiday in York . . . and she knew it wasn't his body that she'd identified. So she came here and forced it out of me. . . ."

" Does he know his wife has found out ? "

" Yes, he came just after she'd left and I had to tell him."

" What did he say ? "

" Not very much. He didn't mind sharing the money. Half would be enough for him . . . so long as he wouldn't have to live with her again."

" Did you tell him what I'd said on the phone ? "

" No, he went off before I had a chance. What does it matter now, anyway ? Everything's finished. He'll never get that new start in life, now. . . ." Miss Scott clenched her skinny hands and beat them on the arms of her chair in sudden impotent anger. " That woman and her brother ! Even when Frank had broken free of them at last, they couldn't let him alone."

Something in her voice set off an alarm at the back of Piper's mind. He said, " Where did Frank say he was going when he left here ? "

She put both hands to her stomach and her face twisted with pain that took her breath away. When she managed to speak, she said, " What do you care ? Your job is done. It's no business of yours to hound him. Let the police do—"

" I don't want to hound him, Miss Scott, but I'm afraid of what he might do. He still thinks the Cresset will pay out . . . and he must know that Alice Mitchell won't be content with half the money. She hates him too much to let him have his freedom and five thousand pounds. She's got him trapped . . . and he knows it only too well. Don't you understand ? "

Very faintly, Miss Scott said, " Yes . . . yes, I understand. But what can I do ? Everything's finished . . . God help him . . . everything's finished. . . ."

There was no room now in Piper's mind for anything but an overwhelming sense of conviction. He said, " You can help him . . . and so can I. But there isn't much time. You must tell me where he went."

She looked up at him dully. In a dry voice, she said, " He told me he had to talk to her, make her swear she'd leave him alone after she got her share."

" Does that mean he was going to follow her home to Richmond ? "

" Yes. She said she was going home when she left here, so he—" Her mouth remained open while she watched him go to the door.

As he went out, Piper said, " Alice Mitchell's a stupid woman. I don't think she has enough sense even now to realise that a man can be driven just too far."

CHAPTER XXI

THE WIND had dropped and there was a threat of rain in the air. Douglas Crescent was quiet and deserted under a lowering sky.

He told the taxi driver not to wait. As he pushed open the gate of number 9 he thought he caught a glimpse of someone peering through the curtains of the house next door.

There seemed to be no one at home in the house where Frank Mitchell had once lived. Piper stood and listened while he asked himself if he had allowed his imagination to run away with him.

. . . *If she didn't go straight home, he'd find no one in. . . . So he'd go away and decide to come back later. If I get in touch with the police now, they can be waiting here for him when he returns. Whether Alice Mitchell is in any danger or not. . . .*

That was when he discovered that the front door had not been shut properly. At the pressure of a finger it swung open a few inches and he could see the empty hall . . . the flight of stairs leading up into the dimness of the floor above. In the hush that filled the whole house he could hear the rhythmic ticking of a clock.

. . . *The latch might not have engaged properly when she went out to visit Miss Scott. If she'd been in a hurry it's the kind of thing that easily happens. . . . But why should she have been in a hurry? Not that the reason is important. You can easily find out whether she's come home or not. Just ring the bell or knock. . . .*

Ring the bell . . . or knock. . . . There was something wrong with the idea of making a noise in this silent house—any kind of noise.

He pushed the door open wide and went on listening and thinking, thinking about a man whose attempt at escape had failed. Alice Mitchell and her brother had proved too strong. A trick of fate that afternoon when Newton's turn of duty had been switched made sure there would be no escape for Frank Mitchell.

When a woman had lived with a man for fifteen years she knew him better than he could ever appreciate—even a stupid woman like Alice Mitchell. She had trapped him into marriage ; now she would rob him of every penny she thought the insurance company was going to pay Miss Scott through the terms of that second will.

Women like her possessed cunning, but no imagination. They were unable to put themselves in someone else's position, to realise what someone else might have to do.

On the floor above something creaked . . . like a floor-board . . . or the spring of a chair. . . . It was only a minute sound that could have meant nothing. Then the house was still again.

From the main road came the hum of traffic, the far-off whine of a car accelerating in low gear. At the farther end of Douglas Crescent somebody whistled as he walked, footsteps striking the pavement sharply. In the distance a dog barked and he could hear a woman's chiding voice.

Then the sound on the floor above repeated itself. He took a step inside the hall and called out, " Anyone at home ? "

Nothing stirred. The silence was the silence of a house in which no one had ever lived.

. . . This was where hatred had grown like a festering sore through the years. This was where she destroyed his life—or he destroyed hers. Just as it took two people to make a quarrel, the seeds of a woman's hate flourished best in the soil that a man had tilled.

Her words made a hollow echo in Piper's mind : ". . . *I hated him. I should've killed him before he had time. . . .*"

She had spent six months in a retreat. Whose fault had that been ? Perhaps she had been as much sinned against as sinning. Who was to judge ?

He took another step and called out again, " Hallo ! Anyone at home ? " Then he began to climb the stairs.

There was no sound from the floor above, no sign that he was not alone in an empty house. Yet when he reached the landing he had a chill awareness that someone or something was waiting for him. In the grey light from the window at the turn of the stairs he stood and flexed his hands and strained to hear the slightest noise.

To his left there was an open door beyond which he could see part of a half-tiled bathroom. In front of him another door revealed one end of a bedroom: a rectangle of carpet, a wardrobe, a bed on which lay a coat that looked as if it had been tossed carelessly on to the bedspread.

He stood without moving while the clock downstairs ticked off ten slow, deliberate seconds. Then he forced himself to move. On legs that had lost all feeling he walked stiffly into the bedroom.

The curtains were half-drawn and they let in only a little light from the drab grey sky, but that light was sufficient for him to see clearly what he had only been able to glimpse while he stood outside on the landing.

It was a man's coat, a belted raincoat made for a man of more than average height. But it was not long enough to conceal completely the woman who lay full-length across the bed. Her feet and ankles stuck out.

. . . Dark stockings . . . black shoes with low heels. . . . Alice Mitchell had worn shoes like those the last time he had seen her. She was a small woman, too. It could scarcely be anybody else. . . .

He went round to the other side of the bed. With clumsy fingers he lifted one end of the coat just enough to let him see what lay underneath.

It was worse than he had anticipated—much worse. This was one of those terrible things that return to haunt a man's dreams for a long time. This was the final expression of all the vileness that had been fomenting below the surface in the quiet house at number 9 Douglas Crescent down through the years. This was the end to which hate had led Alice Mitchell.

He felt sick as he released his hold on the coat and let it cover her again. The pain in his mind was greater than any physical revulsion. He wanted to get away, to get out of this house and into the fresh air of sanity, to step out of the nightmare that had begun one summer's evening when Frank Albert Mitchell took his dog for a walk.

His job was done. The police would know what to do next. . . .

A floorboard grunted on the landing. He moved away from the bed and took a short pace towards the wardrobe so that he could see out of the bedroom doorway. Then he went quite still.

A man was standing there watching him, a man with grey hair going thin and meek, negative features. The light from the window behind him shone on the open blade of the razor he held in his right hand.

With a little apologetic cough, he said, " I hope I didn't startle you." His voice was negative, too.

Piper said, " I called out twice before I came upstairs. I thought there was no one at home, but I felt I ought to make sure—just in case. You understand . . . don't you ? "

He had to make conversation, foolish or not, while his mind worked frantically to find a way out. He had walked into a trap. Now there was no going back. The only route was blocked by a madman with a razor in his hand.

. . . He must be mad. Only a maniac could've done what he did to his wife. . . . The chair beside the bed looks too flimsy to be of much use, but it might hold him off long enough. . . .

The man in the doorway said, " Yes, I do understand. You don't need to apologise. I heard you calling from the hall while I was in the bathroom."

" When I got no reply," Piper said, " I took it for granted you had gone. If I'd thought for a moment you were in the bathroom I'd have waited downstairs."

. . . Keep him talking. It's your only chance. Don't mention her. . . . If you can keep the bed between him and yourself. . . .

In a tired voice, the man in the doorway said, " It doesn't matter. Somebody was bound to come up sooner or later. I was just going—out."

He glanced at the bed and then he put a hand to his face as though it hurt. " You've seen what I did . . . haven't you ? "

There was no purpose to be served by denying it. To

pretend might do more harm than good. Piper said, " Yes, I've seen her. Why did you do it ? "

" I—I had to." With his eyes on the bed he came a few steps into the room. Then he looked down at the razor in his hand. He said, " I suppose I ought to feel sorry . . . but I'm not. She drove me to it. Did you know her ? "

" Yes. She came to see me about the insurance policy. My name's Piper. I'm working for the Cresset Insurance Company."

" Oh, yes." He sounded as if he were merely being polite. Piper's name meant nothing to him.

After a short pause he came nearer still. The pupils of his eyes were wide and demanding. He said, " Do you know what she did ? "

" No. If you'd like to tell me about it, go ahead. I'm just sorry that you found it necessary—to kill her."

" She made it necessary. She wouldn't "—he wiped his hand across his mouth—" she wouldn't leave me alone. I came here to ask her if she'd let me have half the money like she'd said she would. If I had that I could go away and start a new life. It wasn't much to ask, was it ? "

. . . If there's time to grab that chair and smash it over something, one of the legs will serve as a cudgel. . . .

" No, I don't suppose it was," Piper said. " But I expect she wanted the lot ? "

" Yes. She laughed when I begged her not to do it. She taunted me. She said she'd make me pay for what had happened to her brother. I swore to her that Jim's death had been an accident, but she wouldn't believe me. She wouldn't stop talking about how she was going to make me suffer. She wouldn't stop . . . it did something to me inside my head. . . ."

He came another step nearer and stared down at the bed with an empty face. " At last I couldn't stand it any longer. I got hold of her and I put my hands round her throat . . . but I wasn't strong enough. She struck me and got away. . . ."

His eyes drifted here and there and finally came back to the razor. " So I went and got this from the bathroom.

When I came in here she didn't see what I was holding. She called me a coward and a weakling. She said I wasn't even strong enough to choke a woman. Then she dared me to lay a hand on her once more . . . and she turned her back on me. . . ."

"I know how you must've felt," Piper said.

"Do you? I wonder if anyone will ever know." With slow careful movements he stropped the shining blade of the razor on the palm of his left hand while he stared at Piper doubtfully. He said, "She left me no choice. She went on talking . . . horrible things . . . really horrible things. So I came up behind her"—he took a deep breath—"and I cut her throat."

The distant traffic noises belonged to a different world. Reality had ceased to exist in number 9 Douglas Crescent.

Piper said, "What're you going to do now?"

"Do?" He shook his head. "What d'you think I should do?"

"Well, I suggest first of all that you put that thing away. Then we can talk it over."

He closed the razor and opened it and closed it again. Without any feeling, he said, "I should've used it on myself . . . but there was her blood on it . . . her blood all over my hands. . . . When I'd washed them clean I hadn't the courage to do it. . . ."

His face crumpled. In a broken voice, he said, "She was right . . . God help me, she was right. I'm not a man. I've been a failure all my life. Now I haven't even got the guts to do the only thing that's left for me to do."

"Give me the razor," Piper said. "Don't think about her any more."

"Will you tell the police—what's happened?"

"If you want me to."

"Yes, please. I wouldn't know what to say."

"All right, I'll tell them," Piper said. "Then they'll take her away and you can forget all about it. Now, let me have the razor."

"No . . . no, you don't understand." He came one more step closer, his mouth working, the razor open again and held against his chest with the blade uppermost. " I don't want them to take her away. I don't want. . . ."

The razor dropped from his hand. Like a man stricken blind he groped his way to the bed and put his arms round the shrouded body of his wife. Then he began to mumble over and over again, " Don't take her away . . . don't take her away. Please . . . I didn't mean to do it. Please, don't take her away. . . ."

His grief exhausted itself at last. He got up off the bed and turned to Piper with a strange calm in his face. He said, " Do you know Miss Scott ? She lives at Forest Hill."

" Yes, I've visited her a couple of times," Piper said.

" Will you be seeing her again ? "

" I can make it my business to do so."

" Then will you give her a message for me ? "

" Of course. I'll be only too pleased. What is the message ? "

" Tell her—" He looked down at his hands as though they still felt unclean. When he had put them out of sight behind his back, he began again. " Tell her I'm sorry. Give her my love and my gratitude—for everything." His eyes filled with a new resolve as he added, " And say good-bye for me."

" I'll do that," Piper said. " Are you ready to go now ? "

" Do I have to go with you ? Can't I stay here and wait for the police ? "

" If you prefer that . . . but wouldn't it be better if you came with me ? This house is no place for you."

" Oh, I'll be all right." He took one last look at the bed and then he walked out on to the landing.

When Piper joined him, he said, " I'd like to make myself a cup of tea . . . while I'm waiting. There'll be time for that, won't there ? "

" There'll be plenty of time," Piper said.

" Thank you . . . thank you very much."

As he began to go downstairs he looked back. In a small, grave voice, he said, " I promise you I won't cause any trouble. I'll be here—when they come for me. . . ."

CHAPTER XXII

THEY FOUND HIM lying on the kitchen floor with his head resting on a cushion inside the gas oven. He had not been dead long.

Detective-Superintendent Mullett was annoyed. He said, " I'd have expected a man of your intelligence to show a little more sense. Didn't the thought strike you that he might do something like this ? "

Piper said, " You'll find the answer to that question in the Book of Genesis. In other words, I wasn't his keeper. What he chose to do was not my responsibility. Anyway, the letter he left should help you to tie up the loose ends of this affair without much trouble."

" That's as it may be. Your duty was to stay here with him until I arrived."

" Was it ? If I did have any choice, I prefer to think I chose the better course. I remember learning at school that line from Othello where Desdemona says : '*I do perceive here a divided duty.*' "

The superintendent looked at him and grumbled, " They should also have taught you that the devil can cite Scripture for his purpose. However—" he shrugged and turned to Sergeant Pugh—" I think there's nothing more for us to do here . . . and I've a feeling that Mr. Piper expects us to give him a lift back to town."

Pugh said, " Well, there's a spare seat in the car, sir."

" He deserves to walk, if you ask me. . . ."

They went out to the car. As Mullett opened the rear door, Piper said, " You've known for some time what must've happened that night . . . haven't you ? "

With a smile not far from his eyes, Mullett said, " If you mean, did I suspect, the answer is yes. There had to be some good reason why a man should leave so much money to a woman who had only a few months to live. When Mrs. Mitchell identified the body, I thought I'd have to get myself some new ideas . . . in spite of Newton's death and the fact that the pathologist didn't find any fragments of optical glass embedded in the face of the man we fished out of the Thames. . . ."

When they got into the car, Piper said, " I forgot about the spectacle lens. Was that the secret you wanted to keep to yourself this morning ? "

Mullett said, " Yes. I also didn't tell you I'd asked the police at York to scour the town and surrounding district for a man who answered the description of our late friend."

As the car pulled away from the kerb, he added, " What I didn't expect was that he might've returned to London."

" Supposing you wanted to go and live somewhere under a false name ? If you had no National Insurance card, how could you get a job ? "

" No difficulty on that score. I could say I'd just come over from Ireland. The local authorities would issue me with an insurance card . . . and there's plenty of casual farm work to be found in Yorkshire at this time of the year. During the few months it would take Miss Scott to collect, he could lie low quite comfortably."

" And when she died the truth would die with her," Piper said.

Superintendent Mullett grunted, " Perhaps there is a destiny that shapes our ends. Who could have anticipated that James Newton would make a chance trip to York ? If those two hadn't met that night . . . if Alice Mitchell hadn't been so anxious to have her husband disposed of. . . . Dear, dear. . . ."

From the front seat, Sergeant Pugh said, " If you don't mind me making a comment, sir. . . ."

" Not at all, Sergeant. What is it ? "

" I was just thinking about that Mrs. Coupland, sir. Maybe she was knocked down, after all. Did you find any mention of it in the letter he left ? "

" No, but I'd say she probably did see him . . . even if she dramatised the incident because she's that kind of woman."

Piper said, " There isn't much doubt that he swam across the river, stripped off, and changed into dry clothes. Some time during the night, or early next morning, he took a train to York. If the plan had gone wrong for any reason, he only needed to stick to his story that he'd been attacked and had lost his memory as a consequence. He'd committed no serious crime . . . until he came face to face with Newton in York."

Over his shoulder, Sergeant Pugh said, " I don't suppose anyone will ever really know what took place between them that night." His heavy face hardened. " One thing sticks in my throat. I don't keep a dog myself, but how he could've treated that poor little fellow the way he did beats me. He doesn't seem to have been the kind of man you'd expect to behave like that."

" Alexander was her dog," Piper said. " There can be no other explanation for what he did. He couldn't have done it otherwise. I know—I spoke to him."

Mullett said, " You were lucky not to get your throat cut, too, my friend. Next time, don't go walking into people's houses uninvited."

" If I can help it there won't be a next time," Piper told him. " I don't mind admitting I got the biggest scare of my life when I saw him standing outside the bedroom door with a razor in his hand . . . especially when I'd just seen what he'd done to her."

" Yes, nasty business, nasty business all round. However clever they think they are, they always get beyond themselves. His own blood on the handle of the walking stick and the cap . . . more of it on the broken spectacles. And he took away part of the right lens to complete the picture. Planned the whole thing down to the last detail. Trouble with a scheme of that kind is that there's always the temptation to try to improve on it. Dear, dear. . . ."

Piper said, " As you say, a very nasty business. Consoling to think that a little good might come out of it all."

" Such as what ? "

" Two young people will get their chance to find happiness together perhaps sooner than they expected. The Cresset won't be ungenerous in the circumstances."

The superintendent nodded and smiled fleetingly. " That young fellow, Kenneth, is Smart by name and smart by nature. He spotted the one thing we should all have seen long ago—the thing that sent you back to question Miss Scott again. Without it she'd never have been driven to blow the gaff . . . once Alice Mitchell's mouth was shut."

A picture of Miss Scott came into Piper's mind. To have her prosecuted for her part in the affair was unthinkable. . . . He said, " I don't know what you mean. She didn't tell me anything."

Superintendent Mullett pulled down his brows and shifted position. In a grumbling voice, he said, " I was under the impression that you told me—"

" You were under the wrong impression," Piper said. " So far as I'm aware, Miss Scott had no part in it."

" I see. . . . That's the attitude you're going to adopt, is it ? "

" It's the only attitude I can adopt."

" But you know perfectly well what she intended to do with the insurance money."

" Do I ? All I know is that Frank Mitchell left her ten thousand pounds in his will. How she meant to dispose of it is a matter of conjecture. Of course, if you feel that you ought to charge her with conspiracy, don't let my opinion stop you."

After a long silence, Mullett said, " You're a sentimentalist. You know that, don't you ? "

" So I've been told."

" It'll get you into trouble one day."

" I've been told that, too."

In a remote voice, the superintendent murmured, " Perhaps you're right. The news she's about to receive will do more to her than any punishment the law could inflict."

Piper said, " Now, who's being a sentimentalist ? . . . Would you drop me at the next corner, please ? I can catch a train from there. I want to pay my final visit to a house in Forest Hill."

THE END